Ghost Boy

Ghost Boy

Stafford Betty

OUR STREET
BOOKS
Winchester, UK
Washington, USA

First published by Our Street Books, 2018
Our Street Books is an imprint of John Hunt Publishing Ltd., No. 3 East St., Alresford,
Hampshire SO24 9EE, UK
office1@jhpbooks.net
www.johnhuntpublishing.com
www.ourstreet-books.com

For distributor details and how to order please visit the 'Ordering' section on our website.

Text copyright: Stafford Betty 2017

ISBN: 978 1 78535 798 5
978 1 78535 799 2 (ebook)
Library of Congress Control Number: 2017946568

A CIP catalogue record for this book is available from the British Library.

Design: Stuart Davies

Printed and bound by CPI Group (UK) Ltd, Croydon, CR0 4YY, UK

We operate a distinctive and ethical publishing philosophy in
all areas of our business, from our global network of authors to
production and worldwide distribution.

Chapter 1

THE GIRL

The Miller twins, Paige and Penelope, were giving a 1950s birthday party. Ben Conover, like the twins, turned twelve on the same day. But unlike them, he kept it to himself. He was used to keeping secrets.

Mrs. Miller, the twins' grandmother and hostess, was the inspiration behind this strange party. She said she wanted "the kids" to understand what life was like when she was their age. She made them check their phones at the door and line up to play Musical Chairs.

"Oh my God, what is she thinking?" the kids whispered.

In desperation she gave up. "All I ask," she said, "is that you all stay together, boys and girls, and play together whatever you choose. None of this breaking up into groups and cliques!"

For a while they couldn't make up their minds, but when Sung Lee suggested Spin the Bottle, everybody was so amazed they were stunned into agreement.

"You've played Spin the Bottle, Sung?" Tyler Slocumb asked in disbelief.

He had. Sung asked everyone to sit or kneel on the thick Persian carpet in a great circle under the atrium, girls and boys alternating. Then he asked for a bottle, and Mrs. Miller produced a Coke bottle from a collection her husband had. It was an ancient green thing with the name of the city where it was manufactured, "Boston," embossed on the bottom.

"No genie would camp out in that bottle," joked Nick

1

Fitzhugh, who was famous for making squeaky noises in math class by inserting his finger into his mouth and blowing out.

Half of the kids were familiar with the game, but Ben and some of the others had never played it. After Sung explained it, the Duffer said, "I'm not gonna do that!" And Caleb said, "Lemme outa here!" But secretly they were up for it.

"You mean I have to kiss Brad!" said Tyler.

Mrs. Miller suddenly stepped in and set up the rules.

"No, no, Tyler. I played this game when I was a girl. If the bottle points at another boy, you spin again. Unless you'd like to kiss him!"

"Uh—no thanks!"

Everybody laughed, and trendy Melissa Braywith, who sometimes claimed she was neither male nor female, but "transgender," whispered to Tyler sitting next to her, "Maybe she's cooler than we thought."

"Suppose you don't want to kiss the girl!" said Jared, Ben's best friend.

"You have to," Mrs. Miller said. "You chose the game, and you have to play by the rules."

"How long do you have to kiss her?"

"Just a smack, that's all you're allowed. I'll be watching!"

"How long can she kiss me?"

"Nobody'd want to kiss you, geek breath!" Brianna Alvarez broke in.

"All right!" said Mrs. Miller. "Somebody has to go first."

The boys hooted as they pointed fingers at friends. The girls sat quietly or giggled. Their faces telegraphed a full range of emotions, from nervous enthusiasm to disgust.

Ben watched with interest as the game unfolded. He was ashamed to admit it, but he had never kissed a girl except his big sister, and he wondered what it would feel like.

Round and round the bottle spun. *Vwizzzzzh.* Then it stopped, and boy kissed girl and girl kissed boy. When Neeru Patel spun the bottle, it pointed at Ben. She got up, knelt in front of him and studied his face for a second. Then she snapped her face forward and kissed him on the mouth. Man, there were some serious catcalls and yowls. "Wooooo! Woooooooo!" Ben's face lit up the room.

Now it was Ben's turn to spin the bottle. Who knew what each girl was feeling? He thought of the way he looked in the mirror at home: curving high forehead, square jaw, glowing dark eyes, skin a little darker than he'd like. Was he good looking? He had his doubts. He thought of his reputation at school: a little weird but a good athlete, and he could draw with a great likeness. He was respected, but only because he kept his great secret tightly bottled up. Anyway, one of the girls was about to get kissed by him. Would she like it? Would she dread it? He had no idea. He spun the bottle.

The bottle settled and pointed straight at Jared.

Ben got up and made a rush for him. Jared rolled into a ball on the floor and yelled, "No way, dude! Freak! Freak!"

As the laughter died down, Ben spun the bottle again. It pointed at Penelope. He gently kissed the birthday girl on her delicate, freckled cheek.

The game went along smoothly until Tyler spun the bottle and it pointed to a girl Ben didn't know.

"Oh, Pam, lucky you!" said Mrs. Miller. She then spoke to all the kids. "Maybe some of you didn't meet the twins' cousin, Pam Grady." She turned back to Pam. "Pam, this is Tyler. I'm told he's a great athlete."

Pam had small squinty eyes, chubby cheeks, and a weak

chin. Some would say she was homely, not a proper match for a star football player. At least Tyler didn't think so.

"Uh, I think I'm gonna pass, Mrs. Miller."

"Now, Tyler, don't be bashful. Rules are rules."

"Uh, I'm not bashful!" he said forcefully, making his meaning very clear.

Dead silence for five seconds. No one said a word, no one dared breathe, not even the perky Mrs. Miller. Her 74-year-old face under silvery hair turned beet-red.

Ben watched it all, and saw the poor girl's lip quiver, her head pointed down at the floor. He hated what Tyler was doing, hated it, hated it! And he wondered—no, he couldn't do it. Then he saw something—a girl standing outside the circle next to the door. He recognized her, he had seen her many times before, he felt like he had known her forever but didn't know from where. He looked around just to make sure no one else saw her. Of course they didn't. They never did. He looked back. She was just staring at him. It was as if time had stopped. Now is your chance, he heard her say, but not out loud, not even in words. Then she faded away.

"Mrs. Miller, can I take Tyler's place?" he said in a trembling voice.

"Oh, Ben, oh, Ben, would you? Would you!?" Turning to Pam, she said, "Pam, Ben seems to have taken a shine to you."

There were a few chuckles and nudgings, but no one said a word as Ben, paralyzed with embarrassment, got up and walked across the circle toward Pam. When he stooped down and she looked up, her eyes were swimming with tears. He pecked her on the cheek, which was hot and wet. It was doubtful she even saw who it was.

Chapter 2

THE BASEBALL GAME

It was the last inning of the big game. The Padres were playing the Rockies—the best, the baddest, the cockiest team in all of California. The Padres were behind 4–3, it was two outs, and Justin, slow as a tractor, was on second base. It was Ben's turn to hit, their last hope. The Rockies' pitcher was a tall, gangly kid with a great fastball and a streak of wildness to go with the purple streak in his hair. Opposing teams called him "the Octopus" because of his weird, herky-jerky windup. Ben forgot about everything except surviving as he stepped into the batter's box. *Just get the bat on the ball.*

All around him voices cried out. He heard his dad, the Padres' coach— "Get on base, any way you can!" He heard the other coach's shrill two-fingered whistle, *wheeeeeuuu!*, the Rockies' all-purpose wake-up call. He heard a wall of sound coming out of his own dugout: "You can do it, Ben!" Hands clapped, throats roared encouragement. Someone banged on the dugout roof, and an angry fan yelled at the umpire. Ben even heard his mother shout his name from the bleachers.

Ben sucked in a breath and tried to calm himself. He took a practice swing, another, a third, dug in his left toe, went into his crouch, wiggled his butt, then settled in and stared at the pitcher. His heart beat with hope and fear as he readied his hands to explode forward with the bat. He waited. Finally the Octopus went into his windup, arms and legs flying outward. Faster than a boy can think, the ball sped toward him. He swung the bat, felt the ball knick the underside, glimpsed the ball trickling toward third base and the third baseman rushing in. Then he took off toward first, never looking back. *Whop, whack!* The ball and his foot arrived a split second apart, the foot first. He was safe by a whisker; he had gotten a hit off the Octopus, and Justin had waddled ahead to third base. He felt a thrill ripple through him as the crowd roared.

Now it was Noah's turn at bat, and everybody focused on Noah. Ben watched his dad standing next to third base. There it was — the steal sign. *Dad, what are you doing?!* Ben crouched down with hands out and fingers fluttering, then sprang. Like a torpedo homing in on its target, he zoomed toward second base. He slid headfirst in a cloud of red dust and felt the shortstop's glove spank down on his arm too late. "Safe!" shouted the umpire, and the crowd roared some more. Justin was still on third base. The Padres were still losing 4–3.

Ben got up and dusted himself off.

"Come on, Noah, hit the ball!" he yelled. But what he really thought was that Noah would strike out. He was no match for the Octopus.

Three pitches later, Noah was down to his last strike.

Like air hissing out of a punctured tire, the Padres and their fans watched without hope as the Octopus went into his windup and fired. Then something totally unexpected happened. To everyone's surprise, Noah actually hit the ball. It was a weak grounder bouncing straight to the shortstop, a routine play to end the game. Running at the crack of the bat, Ben slowed down just enough to beat the ball as he ran in front of the shortstop trying to distract him. Then he heard the crowd of moms, dads, uncles, aunts, brothers, sisters and cousins start yelling, *really* yelling. He knew his distraction had worked. The shortstop was bobbling the ball.

As Justin chugged home to tie the game and Ben dashed toward third base, he saw his dad's hands stretched straight up in a full stop posture. But right behind his dad was—what was this?—Uncle Dan, Ben's favorite uncle, dead three years, frantically swinging his arm round and round like a giant windmill and looking toward home.

Ben was amazed but didn't hesitate. He dug his cleats into the dirt and rounded third base as if his dad wasn't even there. He zeroed in on home plate and in the midst of all the noise heard his dad screaming, "Stop! What are you doing!" It looked like suicide to everybody. The catcher had the ball in his mitt and squatted down in front of the plate, just waiting. Like a guided missile Ben slid hard into him, body crashing against body.

"Safe!" yelled the umpire, and the whole place went wild. Ben was dazed and lying in the dust. He watched the catcher pick up the ball, jarred loose by the slide. Then all the boys on his team rushed over toward him with arms raised in triumph and faces wild with victory. They dog-piled him and shouted, "Ben! Ben! Ben! Way to go, Ben! We won, we won!" That's all Ben could make out through the roar. You might have thought the Dodgers had won the pennant.

That night Ben couldn't sleep. Over and over he replayed the last inning in his mind: the thrill of getting on base, stealing second, distracting the shortstop, sliding home for the winning run. There was no question about it: he'd won the game with his daring and his speed. And—and Uncle Dan.

He got up and knocked on his parents' bedroom door. It was hard enough keeping the girl secret, but Uncle Dan? He had to dare it. He hoped his dad would be in a listening mood.

"You should be in bed," said his mother, looking up from her book.

"I know. But I keep thinking about the game."

His father looked up from his book with a scowl, and Ben almost turned around and went back to bed. But he had to get it out. Too many years had passed. He sat down on the end of the big bed with its green and yellow patchwork quilt, made by his mother. He wiggled between his mom's feet.

Sam Conover, a building contractor, was grayish and beginning to bald. He had a short-cropped, neatly trimmed salt-and-pepper beard. He had a youthful, slim body that suggested the self-discipline of an ex-Marine. He looked at his son and felt a mixture of pride and irritation.

Maria Conover was bilingual; she gave piano lessons in their home and did translation work on the side; she had silky black hair with wisps of white at the temples. She had handsome features, tight skin, and clear brown eyes that disguised the anxiety she felt about her son. She adored him more than husband and God put together, and she understood him like nobody else could. At least she thought so. She put her book down on her stomach. A faint smile settled over her face as she studied him with the usual pleasure.

His father was still scowling, but Ben gained confidence anyway. "You know what, Dad?"

Sam looked up and waited.

"When I was rounding third base, I knew, I *knew* I was going to score."

"You were lucky! It was stupid, suicidal. Don't ever run through my sign again. Do you understand?"

Sam paused, then said, "What do you mean, *you knew?*"

"I knew. I just knew. I—I saw Uncle—Uncle—Uncle Dan

waving me home."

"What on earth are you talking about? My brother died three years ago." Sam gave his son a look that could freeze a vampire.

Ben shrank back but managed to say in a faint voice, "Dad, there's no way I could've been out."

Sam glared at him with something like fear in his face. Then he asked solemnly, as if he were talking in church, "What are you talking about, Ben?"

"I saw your sign and was about to stop, but Uncle Dan was waving me on like he knew something. I knew I was going to score."

Maria suddenly sat up. "Are you saying you saw Uncle Dan in a vision?"

"*Vision?*" said Sam.

"No. I mean, yeah. I mean, you know—"

Sam and Maria glanced at each other, and Sam's glance told her he had no idea what to say next. He lifted up his hands and grimaced as if he were witnessing a conversation between two lunatics.

"Are you saying, Son, that you saw Uncle Dan's ghost?" said his mom.

"Yeaah, I uh, you know, I guess you'd call it that. And I have a friend who visits me—"

"Oh for God's sake!" Sam broke back in and picked up his book in disgust.

"A dead friend?" said Maria, trying to stay composed.

"Yeah. But I don't know who she is."

"Dead. You mean she's a spirit—like Uncle Dan."

"Yeah."

"And do you talk to this...girl?"

"Uh, yeah. Not much. You know, not much at all. Sometimes. And she, uh, talks to me."

Sam looked up from his book and said, "Don't encourage this, Dear."

Maria couldn't let the conversation drop. She had grown up in Guanahuato, Mexico. El Día de los Muertos, "The Day of the Dead," was in her blood. Every year just after Halloween she turned the extra bedroom into a shrine to her dead ancestors. She lit candles, brought in flowers, and put up old photos. She cooked a traditional meal and served the ghosts on plates spread all over the floor. You could hear her talking to them through the door. After they had taken their fill, she spooned the food back into the pot and fed the family with the "leftovers."

"Darling," she whispered, "I believe in spirits, you know that, but I don't *see* them. Are you sure you didn't imagine your Uncle Dan?"

Ben thought carefully. "No, Mom, I didn't. Unless I'm crazy."

Sam looked at Maria, then back at Ben, just to make sure they were listening. Then he delivered the official verdict: "He's a 12-year-old boy as normal as a tomcat. Let's stop talking this nonsense!"

Ben jumped up and bounded out of the room without another word.

Chapter 3

THE FLAGPOLE

The day had been hot, easily a hundred degrees, and it still hadn't cooled off much even though the sun was only an hour from setting. Bakersfield was baking.

Ben had just finished eating dinner with his mom and dad and older sister, Sarah, who was 16. He walked at a fast clip, eager to get to Jared's, whose house was on the other side of the park. He always cut across the park when going to Jared's, but this time he noticed some bigger boys hanging around the flagpole.

Ben wondered if he should make a detour, perhaps stay on the street and go around the corner. No, they wouldn't bother him. He decided to go the usual way.

Ben noticed as he got within twenty yards of them that they saw him and were nudging and grinning at each other. Then they—four altogether—started laughing. Ben felt his heart flutter, and he wondered if he shouldn't change directions. Or maybe just take off running. He was the fastest runner in his school; he could outrun anybody if he had to. But for some reason he just kept going. He would pass by them on their right, just far enough to show them respect. He would not look up, hurry his pace, or in any way show the fear he felt.

"Hey, kid, did you vote today?" said the tallest of the boys. He wore a black sleeveless tee shirt over his wiry six-foot frame. He looked like the kind of boy who would step on ants for the fun of it.

Ben slowed his pace and kept looking straight ahead.

"I said, did you *vote?*"

The other boys studied Ben, and one pointed to the red, white, and blue sticker of the American flag stuck to the pocket of his shirt. It said, "I voted." It was Election Day, and his mother had playfully stuck the sticker to his shirt. Ben forgot it was there.

"Hey, hey, where you going? *Hey!*"

Ben stopped, and a smaller boy ran up and grabbed his arm. He felt his scalp prickle.

"I thought you had to be twenty-one to vote," said the boy, who had tattoos on the arm that held him.

"Eighteen, Sidney," said the big boy.

"My mom voted today. What's it to you?" said Ben.

"Did you hear that, Crawfish? He's questioning me."

"I heard it, Dingo."

Ben stood still and stared at Dingo. His eyes sparkled with mischief. No, something worse than mischief.

"Hey, where you going?" he said.

"To my friend's house, over there."

"I got something for you to do first."

"What?" said Ben, trying to sound manly.

"What's your name?" said Dingo, sounding friendly.

"Ben." Ben wondered why he didn't run right at that moment. But he thought he ought to stand up to a tough like Dingo.

Dingo saw Ben's fear. "Hey, Ben, don't get scared. We ain't gonna hurt you, I promise, we're just gonna have a little fun. And you'll have the *most* fun!" Dingo reached out and lightly grasped his arm.

Ben said nothing, but his heart was thumping. He felt a prayer form itself in his head. It was the prayer his grandmother taught him to say when he was afraid. He felt a calm spread over him. But the fear was just underneath.

"See this flagpole here?" said Dingo. "It don't have a flag. Just some rope flapping around. What do you think of that?"

Ben looked up the flagpole. "What am I supposed to think?"

"We thought you being such a good citizen and all that, and wearing your little flag—it needs, you know, a flag." By now Dingo had a firm grip on his arm.

"No way!" Ben snapped back. He looked up with his dark eyes flashing at his taunter and pulled back. At that moment Dingo pulled out a jackknife from his pocket and opened the blade, which flashed in the sun.

"That way you could be, you know, patriotic."

"No way!" said Ben still squirming. "This is stupid."

Dingo held the blade under Ben's chin.

"Did you call Dingo stupid?" said Sidney.

"Shut up, Sid! Get the rope ready."

When Ben looked back at Dingo he saw something that sent a shiver through his whole body, something scarier even than the knife. Spirits he knew, but this was something he had never met before. It clung to Dingo's back and dug its fingernails—or were they claws?— into him. It seemed to be riding him, yes, riding him, but its head was bent down so low that it seemed to penetrate Dingo's.

Ben came back to his senses and tried to reason with Dingo. "What if you let go of the rope?" he said. He looked up to the top. "I could die, you know. This is really not cool!"

"He's right, Dingo," said the littlest boy, who spoke for the first time. "This ain't cool."

"You want to go up instead, Mustard?" roared Dingo.

Mustard scowled and hung his pale shaven head.

Dingo put the jackknife back into his pocket and slid off his belt. He positioned it under Ben's crotch and buckled the ends together. Then he fastened the belt to the clip on the rope.

"Don't do this!" Ben said. He looked at Mustard, and he knew he had at least one ally. *Dear God, protect me!* he cried out inside.

Mustard said something under his breath and scowled.

"Pull!" said Dingo. "Pull! Pull!"

Up, up Ben went. He felt the belt dig into his crotch and grabbed the rope higher up to take the pressure off his butt. He looked down and saw the ground getting farther and farther away from him. In the reflection from a small puddle directly beneath him he saw his body being hoisted up. He noted the spectrum of colors in the puddle, as if a bit of oil was floating in it. His arms and legs bumped against the white pole, scorched from the afternoon sun, and he twisted to keep any part of his body from touching it. Fear grew as he watched the pavement and the boys below grow farther and farther away.

"The human flag!" Dingo sung out. And they pulled on the rope some more.

Ben's arms were tiring as he hung on to the rope. He knew if the boys let the rope go he would fall to the asphalt in a heap. And the asphalt was 25 feet straight down. He wanted to yell for help, but he knew if he did the boys would run, and he would fall. "I can't hold on much longer," he called down.

"Stop your whining like a baby," said Dingo.

"How's the view up there?" said Crawfish with a chuckle.

At that moment a police car sped up. It screeched to a halt, and a voice said over a loud speaker, "THIS IS THE POLICE!

DON'T MOVE!"

Dingo and Sidney dropped the rope and took off running. Crawfish and Mustard were close behind.

Ben threw his hands at the pole to keep from falling. His hands slid down the pole a few feet, then held. A terrible burning scorched his hands, and he was on the verge of fainting and falling. The pain became bearable as he wrapped his legs around the pole and slid down.

"Hey, Ben, grab the rope!" came a voice. It was Mustard. He had come back to help. He grabbed the rope and threw his frail body back, ready to do what he could.

By now the policemen came running up and snatched the rope away from Mustard. "Grab the rope, son. I'm gonna lower you down. Careful!" said the cop.

Ben's hands as he gripped the rope felt scorched, but he hung on until he was six feet from the ground. He let loose and fell into the policeman's arms.

"Was he one of them?" said the policeman, glowering at Mustard as he put Ben on the ground and disentangled his pants from the rope.

"No. Came to my rescue. Water! My hands...burning up!" Ben rushed to a nearby water fountain. "He came to my rescue," Ben shouted back as he let the cool water roll over his hands.

The policeman offered to take Ben to the hospital, but he said no thanks.

That night, lying in bed, Ben wondered about that thing riding Dingo. He tossed back and forth trying to drive it from his thoughts. Had he imagined it? No, it was too real. He forced himself to think of something else. But Dingo kept coming back. Suddenly he had the strangest sense that he was not finished with Dingo, and that this thug was somehow in his future. *Nah. I'll just go the other way next time.*

Just before he woke up the next morning he had a nightmare. There was something standing over him, something that had no face, just a big black hole under a hood where the face should have been. He tried to yell but couldn't. Then the horrid thing pressed against him and held him down, and he couldn't move. Now he was half-awake, but he was still paralyzed, and he couldn't cry out. Gradually he woke up more, and the thing went away, and he got out of bed. His shirt was wringing-wet.

Chapter 4

THE CONFESSION

Sixth grade and some of his friends were history. Two more months, and it would be onward to a new school, junior high. The baseball season had just ended too, and Ben, Jared, and Adam were walking back to the car after the last game.

Ben had to know. If he couldn't trust his secret to Jared and Adam, who could he trust? Jared was a cocky, exuberant, slightly built blue-eyed boy whose real love was video games, but his dad made him play sports. He was famous for his blood-curdling scream—a piercing, throaty war cry that he let fly just before every contest, whether the sport was soccer, basketball, or baseball. His coaches thought it made up for his lack of athletic ability. Ben loved that scream, so full of fun and high spirits. There were reasons Jared was his best friend.

Adam was in some ways an opposite of Jared. In school he was known for his practical mind and was good in math. Cheerful he was not. His parents had divorced the year before, and he had seen first-hand the terrible things that words spoken in passion could do. Ben valued Adam for his interesting mind and his curiosity about the world. And because he didn't say nasty things about other kids. Ever. Adam had brown eyes under a slanting forehead, and he had a bump on his nose. No one would ever call him handsome, but he did not seem to mind. Reserved he was, but not shy. He liked himself the way he was.

How many boys would sit through an entire baseball game

and watch his friend play? Adam had done just that. Such was his devotion to Ben.

Jared was pounding his glove with a ball. Ben carried his special bat over his shoulder. Adam carried only himself.

Earlier in the day Ben had screwed up his courage to feel them out, to risk it. He had a hunch about Adam. There had always been something deep and mysterious about him. He looked back and forth between them now and said, "Do you guys ever talk to someone who's, I don't know—dead? You know, maybe for pretend? Maybe some special person who watches over you—you know, somebody who loves you, like a guardian angel maybe? Someone who tells you things?"

"I talk to my dead dog Simone sometimes," said Jared, "but she doesn't talk back. I just pretend she does, because I miss her." He looked sad.

"No, it's not like that," said Ben. "I'm talking about, like, a real person—a real person who's dead. I mean—who died."

"Are you talking about ghosts?" said Jared. He was suddenly all serious.

Ghosts. Somehow that word didn't quite fit when it came out of Jared's mouth. "Ghosts like you think of them aren't real," Ben said. "But she is. Don't you—?"

"She?... Did you say she?"

It had slipped out. Ben hadn't intended it this way, not quite yet. "Yeah, she's a girl. About our age. She, uh, visits me, uh, sometimes."

"She's a friggin' ghost, Benji! You're kidding me, right? You've got a girlfriend who's a ghost?!"

"She's not my girlfriend." Ben turned to Adam for support. "Adam, you know what I mean, don't you? You have somebody like that, don't you?"

Adam and Ben looked at each other as they walked by the snack bar under the shady mulberry trees. There was a slight frown, something close to a smile but not quite, on Adam's tanned face. "No," he said with simple dignity.

"No? Really? Not at all? Not ever?"

"It sounds like you're talking to ghosts," said Jared. "I've heard about things like that, but I never thought it happened in real life. Do you really talk to a—to a ghost? Jeez!"

"I don't think of her as a ghost. She's an angel. I've even given her a name—Abby."

"And do you see her?" said Jared.

"Yeah, but usually not all of her. Usually just her shoulders and head."

"Wow, that's pretty cool!" Jared paused, then said, "Do you think I could see her?"

Ben had to think about that a moment. "I don't think so." Then he added, "But maybe."

"Could I come over when you, uh, when you might—when you think—when you think you might be, like, seeing her?" Jared's wide eyes glowed.

"I don't think so. I uh—I shouldn't have mentioned it. Look, guys, I don't want you to tell anybody about this. But are you sure? Are you sure you don't have a—have a—a friendly spirit, an angel sort of, who watches over you? I kind of thought I wasn't—I don't know—so unusual."

"I kind of think you're *real* unusual, dude. You're friggin' different, Benji. Hey, what'll you give me if I agree not to tell?" said Jared.

"I'll kill you if you *do* tell!" said Ben.

"I'm gonna tell! I'm gonna tell!" Jared ran out in front of Ben and turned round to face him. "Freak! Freak!"

Ben raised his bat over his head, and the chase was on. They hadn't quite outgrown chasing each other around, and the parking lot provided a special challenge.

Ben was stronger and faster than Jared, so he always got the upper hand eventually, but Jared never minded. It was part of the game for him to get caught. Ben caught up with him between two cars and raised his bat in play as if to give him a good clunk on the head. "OK, I won't tell, I won't tell!" said Jared, panting. "But you're still a friggin' freak!"

"Let's go, boys," Sam called out from across the parking lot. "We've got to get home."

"Hey, good game, Jared," said Sam as the boys walked up. "You got a hit. Your second of the season."

Ben thought to himself, *But I got two hits in one game! Why does Dad always expect so much from me?* Sometimes Ben would almost kill for his dad's approval, but it seldom came. He knew his dad loved him, but still…

Jared and Ben sat in the back seat on the way home. "You know," said Jared under his breath, "You know what, Ben, you're my friend, but you're the weirdest dude I ever heard of."

There was something about the way Jared looked at him that made Ben shrivel up inside.

Chapter 5

THE HOBO HIKE

"Mom, Manny wants to take me and Bernie up into the mountains on a hike. Can I go?"

Of course Maria told him he could go. Manny was Maria's seventeen-year-old nephew, her older sister Carmen's oldest son, an athletic specimen who worked out every day and would begin his senior year in September. He starred at soccer and looked forward to a scholarship to UCLA or USC. His grades had dropped alarmingly the previous semester, but his overall average was still above 3.5. Everybody accepted the explanation Manny gave: He couldn't take his mind off Linda, his first real girlfriend. Ben thought the world of Manny.

Manny's little brother, Bernie, was an eleven-year-old going into the sixth grade. Ben and Bernie had grown up together, taken vacations together, shared the holiday meals, and attended the same church. They hadn't quite admitted to themselves yet that they were growing apart. In particular, Bernie was addicted to video games, but Ben found them repetitious and preferred books.

But a hike with Manny and his friend Ruben—that was something that Ben and Bernie had no trouble at all agreeing on.

"Where are we going?" said Ben. "Can you show me on a map?"

"Don't need a map," said Manny, whose voice hinted at some secret fun. "I know in my head where the treasure is buried."

"Treasure?" said Bernie.

"Yep. We're gonna have us a time." Manny turned his dark dancing eyes under thick eyebrows toward Ben and winked. Then he turned to his little brother. "Don't forget to put Mom's cake in the lunch bag, Weenie."

"Here we are," said Manny. Linda had stopped the car next to the freight yard in East Bakersfield. Long trains rested on sidetracks, two with their lights on and engines running. Manny turned toward Linda in the distance and waved to her. "Wait and see if we get on," he shouted. "If we do, give us two-and-a-half hours from when the train leaves. See you in Tehachapi." She waved back indicating she understood.

"I thought we were going on a hike," said Ben, sitting in the back seat and suddenly very confused.

"We are. On a 'hobo hike.' We're gonna ride the rails."

"You're kidding," said Ben.

Manny turned around and fixed his eyes on Ben. "No, I'm not kidding. Don't worry, we'll be fine. It'll be fun, you'll see. You'll never forget this."

"Is it safe?" Ben would trust Manny with his life, but just the same he wanted to hear Manny tell him it was safe.

"Totally safe," Ruben broke in. "We'll find an empty flat car, then head into the mountains for Tehachapi. We'll get off there, and Linda will be waiting for us to take us back down."

"Wow!" said Bernie.

"Have you ever done this before, Manny?" Ben was still not quite convinced.

"Nope, but Rube has."

"It's totally cool, man, you'll see," said Ruben. "You ever heard of the Tehachapi Loop? Everybody else just looks at it.

You're gonna *go* on it." Ruben—short and muscular, with dark, wide-set eyes and a broad, bristly jaw—was a linebacker on the football team. He exuded physical strength and a solemn self-confidence. Clearly he expected Ben to get the point and line up behind him. Ben found him a little shady.

"Suppose they throw us off," Ben said.

"If they do, they do," said Ruben.

"Then we'll take a hike—an everyday hike," said Manny. "Right, Rube?"

"Right, man."

"That's what your mom—and my mom—think we're doing anyway," said Ben. "Shouldn't we call them?"

"Benji, just trust me, OK? My dad did this more than once when he was a boy, did you know that? Do you think he told his mom? He told her after he got back, you bet. But not before. You know how moms are."

"Yeah, but…"

"Just walk into the yard like you own the place," said Ruben. "Like you take a walk through here every day. Like it's a shortcut home. If you look sneaky, they'll figure out what we're up to and kick us out. When we find our flat car, we'll hide in an empty box car. Then we'll hop onto the flat car as soon as the train starts to move. That's what I did last time and it worked like a charm."

The four walked into the freight yard like they owned the place, Ben bringing up the rear. As they walked on and no one seemed to notice or care, excitement overcame Ben's worry; this was an adventure like nothing he had ever dreamed of. The Tehachapi Loop, yes, he knew about it. Over a hundred years ago one team of railroad workers had started to lay track from the valley floor, a second from the mountain pass, 4,000 feet above. When they met, one end was high over the other. To connect the track the engineers looped the track over itself. Now you could see long trains pass over themselves, the tail of the train riding parallel to the engines. Sam took the family to see the Loop a few summers before, and Ben watched a long train spiral over itself like a rattlesnake moving forward out of a coil. It was something to see, all right.

They found a whole line of empty flat cars and a boxcar on the adjoining track. They hid inside the boxcar and waited for the magical moment. Then there was a loud series of bangs, and the flatcar beside them lurched forward. They jumped out of the boxcar and scrambled up the low ladder leading onto the flatcar and stared out at the world moving slowly by. When the train, now moving faster, reached the crossing, they waved gleefully to Linda. Ben was sure that Columbus experienced no greater excitement when he sailed away from the Spanish mainland for America five hundred years before.

They sped across the valley floor toward the mountains as the warm late-May airstream roared in their ears. Groves of citrus and fields of young corn and grape watched as the happy trespassers clacked their way over tracks that gleamed under the morning sun.

When the train, now halfway up the mountain, stopped on a siding to let a train coming down pass, Ben and Bernie ran forward to a tanker car and began climbing all over it, up and down tiny ladders. They perched themselves on the low railing around the cylinder on top of the car where the oil was pumped in and boldly waved at the engineer of the train heading down. Then they scrambled along the ladders down off the tanker and headed back to the flatcar.

"We're back!" Bernie hollered over the noise. But Manny

and Ruben were bent over something at the far end of the car and did not answer.

"Whatcha doing?" said Bernie as they came up on the big boys hunkered over.

"What's it look like?" said Manny.

They were smoking rolled up cigarettes.

"Isn't that weed?" said Bernie.

"Hey, leave us alone for a little while," said Manny.

The train lurched forward at that moment.

Time began to drag for Ben as the train climbed slowly up the twisting pass. The tunnels seemed sooty and filthy, not exciting and mysterious as they had at first. When they reached the Loop, the engines passed directly over their flatcar; but Ben felt none of the thrill he thought he would.

"Hey, Ben, you won't tell your parents, will you?" said Manny, walking across the car toward him. "Someday you'll understand, cousin."

Ben looked up at Manny, and Manny, even though stoned, knew that Ben was confused. He stooped down and said, "Maybe *you* should try it."

At that instant the girl appeared.

Manny looked at Bernie, sitting beside Ben. "Weenie's tried some, haven't you, Weens?"

"It just made me cough."

"Weenie's just a wimp, Ben. That's why we call him Weenie. But you were the main receiver on your flag football team. I watched you score two touchdowns in one game. Remember?"

"Are you serious?" Ruben broke in. He looked at Ben with new respect.

"Are you kidding, man?" said Manny. "My cousin can run

faster than a jackrabbit. How many touchdowns you say you scored all season, Benji?"

Ben barely heard Manny. He looked intently at the girl. Her face was only a few feet away. That's all of her that was visible.

"What you looking at, Ben?" Manny turned to see what might be there, then back around. "Here, take a puff."

Ben suddenly came back to reality. "No, I don't think so," he said.

Manny's voice became tender and seductive as he bent down very low and put his face inches away from Ben's. "Hey, cuz, have a little drag. This will change your mood. This is good stuff. Hey, hey, look up at me, Ben."

Ben looked up at his cousin and smelled his sweet breath.

"Have I ever done anything to hurt you? Would I hurt you? I just want you to experience the world, that's all. Right, Rube? Here." He laughed as he tried to place the joint in Ben's mouth. But Ben turned his head.

Manny stared hard at Ben, and then stood up. "Just don't tell your folks, OK?" It was true that Manny would never do anything that he thought would hurt Ben, but there was a hint of irritation and threat in his voice.

The train had dragged along at eight or nine miles an hour for much of the climb. But as the tracks leveled a mile short of Tehachapi, it suddenly began to gather speed.

No one noticed until it was almost too late.

"Hey, we gotta jump!" said Ruben.

Manny sprang to life. "Ben, grab the lunch sack! We gotta jump. Here, give it to me."

"I don't know. We're going pretty fast!" He handed Manny the sack.

"We gotta jump. Now! If we don't, hey man, we'll end up in the desert somewhere. We gotta jump! I'm bailing!"

But Ruben beat him to it. He rushed over to the ladder leading down off the car and climbed down. The next thing anyone saw was a body hurdling forward, head over heels. Then Ruben was standing on firm ground behind them, farther and farther behind, waving and shouting at them to jump.

Manny scampered toward the forward ladder with bag in hand. Ben, his heart beating with fear, headed for the back.

It was Ben who jumped next. When his left foot hit the ground, the train was already moving along at twenty-five miles per hour. His left leg acted like a spring when it hit the ground, and he flew forward through the air until his right foot hit, then flew again, though less far. It was the fastest run that Ben would ever take. Then he fell face first and tumbled to a halt.

Ben looked up just in time to see Manny throw over the bag and jump. He hit the ground with both legs and spun out of control. It was hard to say whether he fell head over heels or went into a sideways roll like a carpet unraveling. Manny was already fifty yards ahead of Ben when the unthinkable happened. Ben watched Manny flop over like a ragdoll toward the track, then heard through the roar of the train a scream. Or did he just imagine it? He ran up as Manny rolled back from the track grasping his leg, his eyes bulging and his voice screaming. There was only a stump spewing blood where there had been a foot moments before.

"Oh my God!" said Ruben as he ran up from behind. "Go get help! No, I'll go!"

Ben froze as he looked at the gushing blood, then tore off

his shirt and made a makeshift tourniquet, like he'd learned in the Boy Scouts. "You're gonna be all right," he kept repeating. But Manny only stared up at the blazing blue sky and moaned.

Ben looked up the track toward the little station and saw Linda far away running toward them. He looked for Bernie and couldn't find him anywhere. He noticed that the lunch sack, a dark green plastic trash bag, was just behind him and went to pick it up. The last car roared by, and Ben saw something that turned his stomach: Manny's foot between the rails. He rushed up to it and saw a blood-spattered white sock almost up to the crushed stub that was once an ankle. The top two inches of bone were smashed flat. Ben noticed Linda getting closer, then poured out the contents of the lunch bag on the ground. Whatever else happened, he didn't want her to see the foot. When she reached Manny, now in shock, he had the foot safely wrapped in the bag and out of sight. A few minutes later an ambulance drove up.

The medic ran up and looked at the bleeding stub. "Stop the bleeding!" he called out to his partner. Then he stood up and began looking around. "Has anybody seen the foot? Where is the foot?!"

Ben didn't know what to do but feared the man's anger. What would he want with the foot anyway? He'd probably just throw it away. Ben hugged it to his body and said nothing.

Linda and Ruben stayed with Manny, and a deputy sheriff drove Ben down the mountain all the way to Bakersfield and dropped him off at home. Maria answered the doorbell and brought her hand to her heart when she saw the two of them standing on the stoop.

"He's fine," the sheriff said. "He'll tell you about it."

"Hey, that wasn't much of a hike," said Sam, who walked

up just as the door closed. "It's only three thirty. I thought you'd be gone all day."

"Sam, something's wrong," said Maria. "The sheriff brought him home."

"The sheriff?" He looked with dismay at Ben. "Why?"

Ben placed the sack with Manny's foot on the floor and wrapped his arms around his mother. "Oh, Mom, Mom," he said in a quiet voice.

At that moment their pet dog, a longhaired dachshund named Duster, ran up and began pawing at the bag. Sam, not knowing what was in it, picked it up.

"Dad, no, don't open it!" said Ben, letting go of his mother and grabbing at the bag.

The bag dropped to the floor with a thud.

"Ben, what's going on?"

"Dad, it's… Manny had an accident, and…"

"What kind of accident?!" Maria held her hand to her heart, fear in her dark liquid eyes.

"Mom, can I…can I talk to Dad about this first?"

"I want to know what happened to my nephew!" she yelled.

The dog attacked the bag again, and Maria snatched it up.

"No, Mom!" Ben lunged at the bag and tried to take it from her, but she turned aside, dug her fingernails into the plastic under the knot that Ben had tied, and tore the top off the bag.

"What *is* it?!" she cried, her face contorting with disgust. She screamed when Manny's foot fell out of the bag onto the floor. "My God, it's a…it's a…*foot!*"

That night the family sat at the dinner table in grim silence. Family dinners were a requirement in the Conover household; their father demanded it and tonight would be no different.

Most nights he picked a piece of classical music from his collection of CDs and quizzed Ben and Sarah to see if they could name the composer. But tonight there was no record and no quiz to distract them from the catastrophic events of the day. The silence forced Ben and his family to sit with their thoughts. Sound came only from the clinking of spoons and the occasional sip of water.

Ben replayed the scene in his head over and over again, imagining different scenes where the outcome might have been different. *What if I hadn't…? Maybe if I had…?*

But the thought that plagued him the most was, *Why did this happen?*

He hung his head and stared at his soup. He was afraid to look up and face his family. He was guilty, complicit in the crime. He agreed to go on the journey in the first place. If he'd decided not to go then things would have turned out differently. No one would have gone and this day would have been like any other. Dad would play his Mozart and Manny would have his foot.

It was Sarah who finally broke the silence. She had her father's coloring—greenish eyes and light brown hair—but her mother's temperament. She poked her spoon at the soup, then looked up at her father with eyes blazing. "Dad, I'm angry about this. How could God have let this happen to Manny? What did he do to deserve this punishment? He kicked hundreds of goals with that foot. It was famous. It should be mounted and hung on a wall next to a moose's head! Oh, God, what am I saying? I'm sorry! But why? Why?" She heaved with a sob, then controlled herself.

Ben kept his head down as his father spoke: "Manny was stoned, Sweetie. He shouldn't have jumped. His little brother didn't. Maybe God thought Manny needed to be taught a lesson. You take something away from a child, or maybe you even spank him, like my dad did to me. But Manny's not a child; he's almost an adult. Try to look at what happened as the way God, well, spanks an adult. I know this sounds heartless, but think about it."

"You've got to be kidding, Dad!" Sarah blasted back. "He almost died! He lost his foot for a little weed? His foot? Is that fair?" Sarah glared at her father as if he were an idiot.

The argument continued and each set of words started blending into the next in what became nothing more to Ben than background noise. He continued to stare at his soup. He pulled his spoon out of the bowl for the first time and placed it in his mouth upside down. He often ate his final scoops of ice cream in this way; it was indulgent and it made him feel better. He looked closely at the shininess of his now clean spoon and saw his reflection. He wondered if the person staring back at him was a good person. It certainly didn't feel that way.

Then he saw something else in the reflection of his spoon. It was a light, a fluorescence, then a face, and finally a hand rested calmly on his shoulder. The hand exerted no pressure but he could feel it as a warmth and it comforted him. Soon a face that wasn't his was reflected in the spoon, and thoughts that weren't his own began to enter his mind.

Ben raised his head for the first time and said calmly, "Granny says it was an accident."

"*Granny*?" Sarah said. "Granny's *dead*, Ben! What are you talking about?"

A stunned silence filled the room for a moment. Then Ben began.

"She says it's wrong to think that God planned for Manny

to lose his foot. She says stop making God the 'scape'—
'scapegoat?' God didn't push Manny or make him hit the
ground in the wrong way. God didn't make the train move at
twenty-five miles per hour and God doesn't have his—slow
down please, Granny, you're going too fast!—God doesn't
have his fingers in our lives day to day. But God did make
the universe and the laws that—that govern it. And gave us
free will. Manny made a choice and it was a poor one. He
must own it. God was not angry. God loves Manny and is
heartbroken to see this happen."

Then Ben looked up and said, "That's what Granny told
me, Sarah."

Sarah jumped at the mention of her name and looked at
Ben in astonishment. She moved her mouth as if to speak, but
nothing came out. She just stared at him with big round eyes.

"Granny told you this?" said Sam, almost in a whisper.

Ben nodded his head. "She did."

Sam studied his son and slowly shook his head. It was hard
to tell if his face expressed fear or disgust or pity. Maria quietly
got up and began clearing the table. Sam quietly studied his
son for a few seconds more, then said, "We've got to dispose
of Manny's foot."

Outside in twilight Sam selected the spot. It was under the
tangerine tree in the back corner of the lot. A few years before
he had buried the family cat under the same tree.

"Here, you dig." Sam handed Ben the shovel. "And I want
to tell you what you should have done. You should have
handed over the foot to the medic when he asked—"

"But he didn't care about the foot. He just wanted to throw
it away!"

"Is that what Granny told you?"

"No, but I could tell—"

"Listen to me! He wasn't going to throw it away! He was going to bring it to the hospital so it could be reattached! What you did was unbelievably stupid. Dig."

The shovel cut into the damp, irrigated earth. "So I'm the reason Manny doesn't have his foot." Ben couldn't stifle a sob. Then came a flood of tears.

Sam let him cry—and dig. Finally he said, "You were lucky. The ankle was crushed beyond repair. It would have been different if the cut had been clean, like a shovel. Or a saw. But no, you're not the cause. They'll fix him up with an artificial foot. He'll be okay." He reached over and stroked Ben on the back of his head.

They decided not to call Manny's parents after Ben assured them no one knew he even had the foot. "It'll be our secret," Sam said. "We don't want to add to their grief and confusion by telling them you brought it home. They'll always wonder if…you know…it could split the family."

Ben felt close to his father as they dug. He hated secrets, but this was different. They were sharing something they would never forget and never tell anyone. Sam picked up the foot and laid it in the hole as if it were an avocado pit. No fuss. Just business. Nothing seemed to bother Sam Conover. He was always under control. He made everybody feel safe.

Later that evening Carmen called Maria and told her that Bernie had been picked up in Mojave, a town on the other side of the mountains out in the desert.

"He waited until the train slowed down and jumped off," said Maria as she scolded Ben with her Latin eyes flashing. "He's the only one of you with any sense!"

Chapter 6

LIKE A BOBOLINK ON A REED

Ben loved trees, and it was a good thing he did. He lived in one of Bakersfield's older neighborhoods, and mature trees surrounded the house. One, a massive cedar, frightened him when the wind blew hard out of the southeast. He imagined it toppling over and cutting through his parents' bedroom like a knife as they slept. But he was on good terms with the others—especially the camphors and the stately redwoods along the back fence. They gave deep shade as he sat on the deck with his mom or dad on hot summer days. They had provided lookouts for him and his friends when they played games in their branches when they were younger. Their limbs had received the nails that Ben hammered into them when he built his tree forts. And they were home for many birds—from the tiny hummers that fed on the flowers in his mother's garden, to the hawk that built its nest year after year at the top of the cedar, to the noisy green parrots that fed off dates growing in orange clusters from the date palm. Ben loved his yard, and so did his friends. That quarter acre of forest was their private Eden. When storms passed through, they would come over to rake up the debris, and Sam would barbecue steaks for them.

Now it was midsummer, and Sam had just finished a remodel job. A month earlier, on Ben's birthday, he promised to take him camping and fishing in the Sierras—just father and son. Sam would go to church with the family most Sundays, but he didn't fool anyone. The altarpiece of his religion was his bicycle, a black Trek Madone. And his Saturday bike ride was his Sabbath. With a few friends he'd ride between 50 and 100 miles. It was a real sacrifice for him to do anything else. Ben could hardly believe it was happening.

"If you think our yard is beautiful, wait till you see Hidden Falls," Sam said to Ben as they packed their gear. "Redwoods older than Methuselah all around, and almost no one knows about them. And the trout fishing isn't bad either." He picked out a few lures from the tackle box and wrapped them in a cloth. Then he carefully placed a book on top of his clothing. "By the way, there's a front coming in tonight. It might be chilly tomorrow at 5,500 feet before the sun comes up. Throw in your gray ski sweater and some long pants."

Sam knew the area well. He chose the last campsite down the trail, the one farthest from the parking area—just in case the camp filled. But only a few groups had their fires burning at the upper camp sites when twilight deepened in the gorge. Except for the redwoods that towered overhead twenty-five stories and their lesser cousins, the pines and firs and cedars, Ben and Sam were all alone.

The fire crackled and the cool of the night closed them in. The Tule River twenty yards away whirred by. They heard the rustlings of an animal moving about in the dark over leaves and twigs close by. Ben felt close to his father.

"Dad, what are those sounds?"

"Could be a mouse, a weasel, a badger. Or maybe some kind of bird—an owl or hawk. The ranger said a bear stalked the area a week ago. It could be deer. But you know what I think it is?"

"What?"

"A hungry mountain lion."

"A mountain lion?" Then he heard his father chuckling. "Dad!"

They listened to the river's low hum and stared at the dancing flames. Then Ben said in a pensive voice, "Dad, I wish you and Mom wouldn't fight."

Sam bought much of his clothing at a second-hand store; he hung his pants, shirts, and three dress coats in about six feet of closet space. Maria's clothing spilled over into both children's closets. The night before, Sam and Maria had argued over money.

After a pause Sam said, "It's not very pleasant, is it? But it's part of life."

"I know. But it stinks."

"I think I know how you feel."

A light breeze sprang up, and the sighing of the wind sifting through needles added to the swishing of water below.

"You know what, Dad?"

"What, Son?"

Son. His dad didn't use that word often. Other dads called their sons that all the time. Ben liked that word. "I love it here," he said.

"So do I."

"It's so beautiful. Do you know what I felt like doing on the way up? I felt like hugging a tree. I actually did hug a tree for a minute when I was gathering firewood." He poked the fire with his stick. "I'll never forget that feeling. Have you ever had it?"

Sam didn't answer right away, then said, "Maybe so."

They were quiet for a while. Then Ben said, "Do you know

Adam doesn't believe in God?"

"Really? Probably his folks aren't believers. Kids pretty much pick up their beliefs from their parents."

"I don't."

Sam chuckled lightly. "Ben, what can I say? You're one of a kind."

"And you know what? If Adam ever felt what I feel, he'd for sure believe in God."

"Hmm, maybe so." Sam studied his son poking at the fire with his stick, then reached over and tousled his hair.

Ben slapped at a mosquito.

"Did he get you?"

"Yep, he got me... Dad..." Ben jabbed at the fire with his stick. "Sometimes Mom—Mom worries about—silly things."

"Silly things? Well, she's a woman," he chuckled. "They don't always think like us."

"She's always fussing about what I look like, what I put on, stuff like that. Do you think Mom loves God?"

Sam paused, then said with great care, "Son, your mom loves God. She goes to church. She prays. Of course she loves God. Do you think loving God is a little thing?"

"Sometimes I feel like exploding around Mom. I feel suffocated by her. She's always worrying about me, worrying about nothing. She won't let me ride my bike to school in the fog. Every time I cough she makes me take medicine. If she knew Adam didn't believe in God, I bet she wouldn't let me see him. And remember how she almost made me wear a helmet when I pitched? It's a good thing you talked her out of it!"

"I understand your feeling of being—what'd you say?"

"Suffocated."

"That's a strong word. But remember. Your mom loves you very much. And that's the best thing a mom can give a kid. And I wouldn't worry about Adam."

"What was that!?" said Ben.

Sam grabbed the flashlight and pointed it in the direction of the crashing noise they heard. Ben half expected to see two gleaming yellow eyes wide apart. But there was nothing.

"Probably just a limb falling. Yeah, that's what it was. The wind's coming up. It must be that front coming in." Sam looked up at the trees, then straight up through the hole in the forest at the sky. "No clouds. Look at those stars."

Ben looked up at the Milky Way. "Wooow!"

"That reminds me." Sam got up, went into the tent, then came out carrying two jackets and a book. "Here, put this on." He handed Ben one of the jackets. "I want to read a short passage to you. It's by John Muir, the man who got Congress to make Yosemite a National Park over a hundred years ago. I think you'll like this man. He loved trees even more than you do."

Sam sat back down on his rock next to the fire, put on his reading glasses, and trained the flashlight on the book. "Chapter Ten. A Wind-Storm in the Forest."

In 140-year-old poetic language, Muir described the great trees of the Sierras as they swayed riotously back and forth during a wild windstorm in 1874. "The air was mottled with pine-tassels and bright green plumes, that went flashing past in the sunlight like birds." "Young sugar pines, light and feathery as squirrel-tails, were bowing almost to the ground." Yep, Muir sure enough loved trees.

But what impressed Ben most was yet to come. Muir described how he climbed to the top of a 100-foot-tall

Douglas fir at the height of the storm. "The slender tops fairly flapped and swished in the passionate torrent, bending and swirling backward and forward, round and round, tracing indescribable combinations of vertical and horizontal curves, while I clung with muscles firm braced, like a bobolink on a reed."

"Wow!" Ben burst out.

They sat quietly side by side for a minute or two. Then Sam said, "I've been meaning to ask you. What did you mean when you said Granny told you about Manny's foot? How did you know it was Granny?"

"I saw her."

"You saw her? Where?"

"In the spoon. I saw her face in the spoon. And I felt her behind me, touching me."

"In the spoon? You mean..."

"A reflection. In my soup spoon."

Silence. Then, "Hmm, what did she look like?"

"Not like her old self at all. Like her portrait in the dining room. She was young—and pretty."

"Well, all that tells me is you had a conversation with a phantom, something you imagined, something based on that portrait. I have imaginary conversations all the time. Your mom's always telling me I talk to myself. And she's right. But the people I talk to aren't real. Don't you see?"

"But she was talking *to me*. I was doing the listening. And she was *really there*."

"No, Son, she was not there. We would have seen her if she was. I worry about this habit of yours, you know. I really do. It's crazy. And that girl."

"Dad, I'm telling you, Abby is as real as you and Mom."

Sam dug a stick into the embers and worked it around and around. He stared at the fire as if in a trance. Time passed with no one speaking.

Ben crawled into his sleeping bag just as a bright three-quarter moon cleared the eastern ridge and dappled the ground with patches of light that changed shape with each new gust of wind. He fell asleep thinking of John Muir high up in his tree being flung about "like a bobolink on a reed."

Ben didn't care much for fishing, even for the prized rainbow trout. He preferred rock-hopping, jumping from boulder to boulder with the river rushing by at his feet. If he slipped, it didn't matter. The river in mid-summer wasn't deep. It was a dancing stream carrying the season's last snowmelt, not the torrent that had roared through the gorge two months earlier.

It was fun and challenging hopping from rock to rock, but Ben wished he had someone to share it with. He looked down the river at his dad casting, whipping the line, reeling in. He looked up the river. Water rolled over a small waterfall. Swaying trees reached high into a hazy, cool morning sky. The wind came in waves. He heard it gather momentum up the gorge, then come rushing overhead as it lashed the trees into a frenzy, then fade away downstream. On both sides of the gorge jagged mountains reached up to 10,000 feet. Their almost vertical sides were dotted with trees that somehow managed to get a toehold between crags and eke out a living.

He picked up small rocks and skipped them across a pond where the river was calm and had settled. He relived the conversation around the fire. He could feel his dad's concern, his disappointment, even his fear. Did his dad think he was crazy? How could he make his dad understand? How could he make his dad call him "Son" every time?

He stood on his rock and gazed at his dad fishing. Then he got an idea. Or rather he returned to the idea he got when his father was reading to him.

He chose a young pine about eighty feet tall, one with branches growing close enough to the ground for him to reach. It was easy to climb once he got started: A branch jutted out of the trunk every two feet or so; there were no gaps. He could see the river below. If the branches would stop waving for a minute, he might be able to see his father. But they would not. The wind tore through them, and the tree moaned in protest.

The higher he got, the less he felt love for the tree. It had become his rival, his adversary. It wanted to conquer him, and he wanted to conquer it. He did not feel close to nature anymore. He remembered that he was the son of Sam Conover, and for a moment all he wanted was for this great man, this great father of his, to see him up in his tree, to approve of him, to love him.

The higher he got, the more the tree swayed. He looked up and saw the top, perhaps thirty feet up. He looked down and saw the ribbon of water. For a moment he was afraid, but there were branches all around and below him. They protected him. He was not out in the open. Still, he wondered if he should go any higher.

He reached up to the next branch, pulled himself up, then reached for the next. Then the next. Now he did not look down, only up. He began to feel more than a simple swaying back and forth. A swirling, twisting, gyrating motion was trying to fling him down on the ground like a slingshot. He looked up to the very top. He thought he could go another six feet in safety. Then and only then would he call out to his father.

He remembered the flagpole, how afraid he had been, and how much safer he felt now. His mind told him there was nothing to fear; all he had to do was to place one hand on the next branch and pull himself up. A simple motion, that was all. He was beginning to feel a little dizzy, though, and his sweat felt like ice water. The tree bent and pirouetted as the wind whirred. One more branch. Then one more. That was all. He looked at the next branch, took a deep breath, and reached. He brought up his foot, then the other. One more to go! He reached again, then drew up the first foot. The tree swung and bucked, fighting back. Then he drew up the other. He was ten or twelve feet from the top. He had gone as far as he dared.

He glanced out across the gorge, out at the skyscraping ridge on the other side of the gorge, and tried to steady his nerves. A gust of wind howled through the topmost branches and bowed them far over. He clung to the trunk with a death grip and looked straight down at the rocky earth seven stories down. His mind told him the trunk would not break, but his fear told him it could snap any second. The gust passed over, the tree stood tall again, and he felt a surge of joy. This was an adventure that no one would believe. He decided to sit down on two thin branches and just enjoy the ride. He looped his legs around the trunk and settled into a sitting position, snug and secure. He closed his eyes and dared the wind to assault him again. And it did. The trunk bowed far over again. Back and forth, around and around it flung him, but now he felt a wild ecstasy. "Like a bobolink on a reed," he kept telling himself. He laughed hysterically, laughed until he sobbed with joy and exhaustion. Oh, if only Jared were here! The greatest adventure of his life, and he had no one to share it with! Not even Abby. Where was she anyway?

What was he thinking? His father was just a yell away. "DAD!" But the wind washed his voice away. He waited until it died down. "DAD!" He saw his dad, a hundred yards upwind, stand up and look around. He saw him yell but couldn't hear what he yelled. "UP HERE!" he shouted. "UP HERE!" By now he was so confident of his safety that he let go of the trunk with one hand and waved it. "UP HERE, DAD! UP HERE! UP THE TREE!"

Finally, after a whole minute of waving and shouting, Sam looked in the right direction. He was too far away for Ben to see the look of amazement on his father's face. What he saw instead was his father jumping down off his rock. Long legs dressed in blue jeans hopped from boulder to boulder over the river, then up the other side and out of Ben's view. Then he heard his father's voice. "What the hell are you doing? Get down from there! Down!"

"I'm going to have to be careful about what I read to you from now on. No books on rock climbing or glacier hiking, I can promise you that!" said Sam as he piloted the car down the winding road into the great valley. "That was a foolish thing you did. I want to stress that—a *damn foolish thing*. Why did you do it? Did you think—did you think Granny would protect you if you fell?"

"I—I didn't think about falling—I felt safe."

"You were not safe, Ben? The top of that tree could have snapped off under your weight."

"No, Abby would have showed up if there was any real danger."

"Ben, don't give me that crap!" his father yelled.

"But—but Muir was heavier than me. Right?"

His father was tense and silent, and his jaw worked in and out as his teeth clenched. Then he said, "I used to climb tall trees when I was your age. There was one in particular, an old oak way out in the woods next to a field. One almost as tall as yours, tall enough to kill you if you slipped. I must have climbed it five times when I was a boy. It was the only tree you could climb and see the city from, way off in the distance. There was a gap near the top. You really had to stretch to get to that last limb, where we would sit like eagles. I was one scared kid when I reached that gap. Every time it took an act of raw courage to get past it. And the last time, I didn't."

"You fell?"

"No, but my friend did, and I was just underneath him. He slipped and fell all the way down. It makes me sick to think of it. If he hadn't hit a branch, he'd probably be dead. As it is, he's just brain damaged. He lives in a home for people like him. Do you understand?"

"Yeah. What was—what's his name?"

"It doesn't matter."

"So you were a foolish kid like me. Right, Dad?"

Sam kept quiet as he zigzagged the pickup down the mountain. There was a long lull in the conversation. "Don't tell your mother what you did. It was very, very foolish."

Another secret. "OK."

There was more silence. Then, "You're not going to tell your mother about this, are you?"

"No. I promise."

The experiment had failed. Now he was not only crazy. He was foolish. Ben sat in glum silence the rest of the way down the mountain.

Chapter 7

THE PSYCHIATRIST

Mom and Dad were going at it hot and heavy, not physically—it never came to that—but just yelling. They didn't see Ben come through the front door, and he crept up the stairs to his room. He hated their fights, but he also couldn't help listening in, especially when they concerned him, like this time.

"All right, have it your way," Maria yelled. "You always do anyway. But just make sure he's a Catholic. Just give me that. Just that little bit."

"Okay, he'll be a Catholic. I guess you want him to be a woman too, right?"

"Oh my God, you are so clueless! He has a gift, and you are going to destroy it! A psychiatrist? Oh my God!"

Dr. Clyde Sylvester was not a Catholic psychiatrist, not so easy a thing to find in Bakersfield. He was a friend of one of Sam's biking buddies, and Maria gave in. Sam was sure he was doing the right thing for his son, even if it was costing him. *God, why isn't he more like me? Why isn't he normal?* he thought to himself as he drove to Sylvester's office with Ben speechless beside him.

Dr. Sylvester was a pleasant, likable, mild-mannered middle-aged man with an ample belly, and he insisted that he would speak first to Ben alone. Sam would have to wait in the lobby.

The Doctor read from the chart that Ben and his dad had

filled out. "I see you like to read and to play sports, and your grades are excellent. That's a great beginning."

That's the way it started, but when Dr. Sylvester began to dig in, Ben was leery. He didn't trust this stranger. He knew his mother didn't either. "Ben, I want you to tell me everything you worry about. Everything. I don't care how little a thing it is. Don't hold back. And be assured that it will go no further than you and me. Unless you give me permission to talk it over, talk it over with your parents maybe. Can you do that? Can you trust me? Try to trust me, Ben. Think of me as an overgrown friend, a sort of buddy with a beard." He smiled lovingly at Ben. His face communicated real concern.

It hadn't gone well at this first meeting. Ben was holding back. But at the second, things went better. Again the Doctor tried to reassure him. "Have you thought about the things that worry you the most, Ben?"

Ben finally opened up. "Well, I worry about a lot of things."

"Start with the littlest, then we'll build to the big. How about that?"

"Well—uh—that would have to be—this is really embarrassing—my looks. But there is nothing we can do about that."

"Your looks? Hmm. Where would you rate yourself on a scale from one to ten? Ten is tops."

"Oh, I don't know. Maybe a four."

"Ben, you are so wrong. Wait until you reach an age, or a place, where refinement is prized. You have fine features. You're a nine in the making. Trust me."

"Really?" Ben was not convinced.

"Really. Keep going."

"Well, I worry about Mom and Dad. You won't tell them?"

"Of course not."

"They get into fights, sometimes over money, but mostly over me."

"Over you—can you expand on that? What do they disagree over?"

"Well, lots of things. But right now it's over—over—you know—she thinks I have a gift when I see—when I see spirits. And Dad says I'm hallucinating. She's totally pissed that I'm even here."

"And is seeing spirits one of those things that you worry about?"

"It's the thing I worry about *most*."

"Why is that?"

"It's not just Mom and Dad, it's my friends. My best friend texted everybody that I have a girlfriend who's a ghost. I should never have told him. It was soooo stupid."

"You mean you see a girl—a girl that nobody else can see?"

"I don't see her that much, maybe every two weeks. She's just a real nice girl who died. She visits me for, like, company—sometimes she's a little sad—and I really like her. That's all. But nobody else can see her. Not even Mom. And Dad thinks I'm crazy. And all the kids tease me. They call me 'Ghost Boy.' They ask if I'm gonna take her to Dewar's for a hot fudge sundae. And if I'm gonna take her to the prom. They think it's hilarious, and it kinda is. But it gets old. I wish I could be, you know, normal!"

"Is she the only, uh, spirit you see?"

"No. If I let myself, and I do a few cartwheels or back flips, I can see spirits mixed in with regular people. Like at the mall."

"Cartwheels! Well, that's one for the manual! Where did you learn to do cartwheels?"

"I went to gymnastics class for a year."

"Hmmm. Ben, did the other kids see spirits when they did cartwheels?"

"No. I guess not."

"So you're saying cartwheels bring spirits to you, but not to anybody else."

Ben had to think about this for a few seconds. "No, they just make it easier for me to see them. I don't know why. And really, I can see them anyway—when I—I can't explain it—it's something I do to my mind."

"Ben, getting back to regular people, how can you tell them apart? How can you distinguish regular people from spirits?"

"Oh, regular people, they're just, you know, regular. But spirits, they sort of glide, or you see only a part of them, maybe only the shoulders up, or they're surrounded by a kind of mist, or they might look deformed, maybe you see only half a face. Or you see a regular person walk through them. They're easy to tell apart. For me."

"Are there a lot of them?"

"Not many. Not nearly as many as regular people."

"There wouldn't be any in this room right now, would there?"

Ben looked around. "No."

"Well that's good. After all, this is supposed to be a private consultation!"

"Yeah." Ben smiled.

"Are you afraid of these spirits? I mean, if it wasn't for the kids that tease you and your disapproving dad, would you want to get rid of them?"

"No. They're interesting. Especially my grandmother. She looks over me sort of. And the girl. I'm sure I know her from somewhere, but I can't remember where, and she won't tell me."

"So you actually talk to the girl."

"And to Granny. Yeah."

"Tell me, what does the girl get out of her visits to you? What's her purpose?"

"I've been wondering about that myself for a long time. She seems to show up when I'm about to make a mistake. She's like a guide. But at other times she seems like—lonely, maybe even a little sad. Like she needs my friendship or something. She seems very attached to me. It's hard to say."

There was a pause. Then Ben said, "Doctor, do you think I'm crazy?"

"No. You don't have any of the symptoms of a crazy person. I can tell that just by talking to you, watching your expressions, your eye contact, listening to you. You're a healthy kid with an unusual, uh, sensitivity. It's all rather puzzling."

Then he paused. "I assume the spirits are all good, Ben. I mean, do they ever tell you to hurt yourself, or to hurt somebody else? Do they use filthy language? Are they—and do you hear them like voices in your head, telling you what to do? Perhaps threatening you?"

Ben had to think hard about this, then said, "They are out there, Doctor. And sometimes they do scare me. I saw one sort of attached to a kid who was trying to hurt me. But they don't seem to be interested in me. And there aren't that many bad ones anyway."

"And the voices?"

"I don't hear voices in my head. I just hear voices outside my head, when they speak to me. And when that happens, I see them."

"Really?" The Doctor paused.

"Ben, would you like to break off contact with these spirits? To become normal like every other kid? I can help you do that if you like."

He had to think about this. "To be honest, I don't know. As long as I can keep the girl, I guess."

"Hmm. But cutting off all contact, even with her, would please your dad, right? If it came to choosing between him and her, what would you choose?"

Ben fidgeted in his chair. He hated this choice. But in the end he said, "Yeah, I guess I would have to choose Dad."

"I think that's a wise choice, Ben. I'm going to talk to your dad now. Would you mind going out into the lobby for a minute?"

On the way home Sam told Ben he was relieved by what the Doctor told him. "He just gave me some pills for you to take. He said you were fine."

The next day Ben complained of dizziness. He felt drowsy and a slight tingling in his arms and legs. "I don't feel right, Mom," he said as he came down for breakfast.

The second day he complained he had an upset stomach and a dry mouth. "It's those pills, isn't it?" he said. "I just feel like crap. I feel horrible."

"What about Abby?"

"Haven't seen her. Don't feel good enough to see her. I hope she understands."

"Bring me that bottle," she said suddenly.

Ben went up to the bathroom closet and got it. He brought it down to her.

"Let's see what this stuff is," she said. She studied the label.

"Olanzapine. We're going to find out about this stuff. There'll be plenty about it online I bet."

She was right. "For God's sake, this is an antipsychotic drug!" she told him as he looked over her shoulder. "There it is. See that? It helps to 'reduce hallucinations.' See that? Right there!" She almost poked a hole through the monitor she was so angry. "So that's what your great doctor thinks of your spirits. They're not real. They're hallucinations. Your brain just makes them up. I knew it! I knew it!"

"I don't want to take this stuff anymore. The doctor said I wasn't crazy. I'm just not—he said I had a 'sensitivity.' That was just a nice way to say I wasn't normal like all my friends, right? You know what? I don't want to be normal!"

Maria was about to explode. Sam referred to these moments as her "Latin temperament." She threw her hands up to heaven and moved her mouth without quite getting anything out. Her beautiful eyes blazed with outrage, and all Ben could do was cower and wait for the explosion to work its course. She finally settled down enough to splutter, "This is what you should do. Every morning take one pill out of the bottle and flush it down the toilet. One pill, Ben. Do you hear me? One pill every day. DOWN THE TOILET! And don't tell Dad. I'll deal with him in time. But not yet."

Chapter 8

THE ROAD TRIP

Every other summer the Conovers vacationed in Alabama. Sam had grown up in a small town outside Mobile. His father, Granny's husband, dead for eighteen years, had bought a house on the eastern shore of Mobile Bay in the 1940s, and Sam was now one-sixth owner of it. He could use it for a month as long as he kept it up. Sam, Sarah, and Ben looked forward to these vacations. Maria did her best to fit in with Sam's sizable, rather odd family.

They got a late start on the first day of their journey across the country and found themselves east of Barstow in the middle of the Mojave Desert at eleven in the morning. Sam had been annoyed by Maria's lack of preparation, leading to a late start. The desert was beginning to simmer, and Sam turned on the air conditioner. He ran it full blast—the coldest possible temperature setting at the highest fan speed—for two or three minutes. Then he turned it completely off when it got too cool. He left it off for two or three minutes until it got warm inside, then turned it back on. Off and on the air conditioner went, back and forth, with the temperature constantly fluctuating. He did this for the noblest of reasons: to save gas and "reduce the use of hydroflourocarbons, a greenhouse gas worse than carbon dioxide," he explained. Maria found it ridiculous that the family should suffer because of climate change. But she didn't say anything.

Once Sam waited too long to turn the air conditioner back on, and the car got stuffy and warm. With a quick, jerky movement of her hand, Maria turned on the air conditioner and set the temperature and fan speed at "moderate."

For a moment Sam suffered this insult to his sense of order and thrift and said nothing. Ben noticed his mother's act of defiance and thought trouble might be brewing. "Dad, how hot do you think it is outside?" That's all he could think of to say on the spur of the moment. He hoped to break down his father's building anger.

But all Sam said was, "Why'd you do that?"

"We're roasting in here," Maria said. "Or freezing. Would you please leave it at one setting, like everyone else in the world?"

"Let me explain how it works."

"You've already explained it."

"The compressor works at only one speed. If you mix warm air with the cold air, you waste—"

"I don't care! I just want to be comfortable. Don't we have a right to be comfortable?"

"Sure, but—"

"You must be the only person in the world who runs the air conditioner that way. How can you care more about penguins at the South Pole than your own family?"

Ben knew what fair fighting was, and he knew these words didn't qualify. He was sure his father was boiling, and he dreaded the explosion.

"I'm a little warm, too, you know," he quietly fumed. "We all need to do our part. It's like voting."

He reached over and reset the dial.

She reached over and set it back the way it was.

The fan and air conditioner purred along at the same speed for the rest of the day. Sam and Maria spoke to each other as little as possible. Everyone was uneasy, Ben especially. They got as far as Gallup, New Mexico, and stayed in a motel, all four in one room.

They had to cover 800 miles the next day, so they turned in early.

"It's going to be a long day tomorrow," Sam said. "Good night, everybody."

"Good night, Dad," said Sarah and Ben at almost the same time.

"Night, Mom," said Ben.

"Night," she said sadly.

He settled into his bed and heard her sniffling. He knew she was crying, and he wept inwardly for her. *Dear God, please help Mom be happy,* he prayed. Over and over he prayed that prayer. The next thing he knew his dad was jiggling him and telling him it was time to get up.

The cool air rushed by at 75 mph as the van sped across the stark but beautiful high country, home of the Navajo, Apache, and Zuni tribes. On another day the family might have been admiring the great flat-topped mesas that rose in the distance, talking about Indian history or chattering about the breakfast that Maria prepared in the back seat. The brilliant orange sun had just cleared the distant hills to the east, but the glum mood of the previous day hung over each member of the family like a shivery fog. Mom and Dad were not speaking to each other.

"See those mesas ahead?" Sam said to Ben, who was sitting beside him on the front seat. "One of them is the place where the Acoma Indians built a pueblo. Not so much as a blade of grass up there. But such was their fear of the Navajo and Apache, who greatly outnumbered them. That's the only place they could survive."

"How did they get up there, and how did they eat?" said Ben.

"They grew their crops and hunted on the plain below. They captured rainwater in cisterns on top. They got up the mesa along a natural stone stairway. When they were pursued by their enemy... Look!"

Sam pointed suddenly not at a mesa, but the pickup in front of them. Ben looked up just in time to see it hit the shoulder of the road on a curve and flip over. It tumbled over and over, glanced hard off a rock, and came to rest on its roof far off the road.

"What is it, Sam!?" Maria said, lurching forward in her seat.

"An accident. We're going to have to stop. Damn!" He looked in his rear view mirror. There was no one behind. A car with its headlights still on sped by on the other side of the median. "Yeah, we're going to have to stop... This may not be pretty."

Sam pulled over on the paved shoulder and got out. A white pickup truck thirty yards off the road lay on its top, its tires spinning. Dust hovered around it. He bounded down a small decline and yelled back, "Sarah, get help!"

"Get help? How, Dad?" Her voice shook.

"Call 911. And wave down any car that comes along. They might help."

She looked behind her down the road at a car a long way off. "I can't do that!"

"Go ahead, Sam. I'll take care of it!" said Maria.

"Ben, come with me!"

Father and son ran over to the truck and looked inside the smashed open door, which barely hung on its hinges. No one

56

was there. They looked around. "Over there!" Ben said. He pointed to a man lying on his back across some rabbit brush. They ran up to him.

"Look around. There might be somebody else," Sam said.

Sam stooped over the man and examined him closely. He couldn't have been much over twenty. He looked Indian. Blood drooled out of his mouth, ear, and scalp.

"No one else," Ben said, running up.

The man had his eyes open and was alive. But he didn't seem to know where he was.

Sam held the man's hand and said, "We're getting help. Hang in there."

Ben, on his knees, said, "What's your name?"

"Why me?" said the man in a feeble, slow whisper. A rattling sound came out of his mouth when he breathed. "Why me?"

"What's your name?" Ben repeated, his face just inches away from the man's face.

"Alvaro."

Ben looked up, looked back down, then said, "Alvaro, there's a man here. Do you see him?" Ben lifted Alvaro's head ever so slightly. "Do you see him?"

"I'm going to die. Why me?" Alvaro moaned.

"Alvaro, the man is reaching out. He's an old man. Who is he?"

"Dad, help is coming!" Sarah shouted from the shoulder.

Ben continued propping Alvaro's head. "Look, he's right there, reaching out to you. I think he—knows you."

A light flickered in Alvaro's eyes. "Grandpa... Grandpa..."

Ben saw a joy in Alvaro's face, felt him try to get up, then fall back. The rattling stopped, and the old man disappeared in thin air.

Sam felt his pulse, first one wrist, then the other. Finally he said in a hushed voice, "He's gone."

A couple of other people ran up, and one said, "How is he?"

"He rolled his truck, and he fell out," said Sam. "It crushed him. He wasn't wearing a seatbelt."

"My God! Just a boy."

"An ambulance is on the way," said a woman. "Here, I'm a nurse." She got down on her knees and felt his pulse.

"I think it's too late," said Sam.

Ben didn't see any of this. He had withdrawn twenty yards from the scene and was sitting on the ground next to a cactus. He was in his own world.

It was in early December, seven months before, and the family had taken Granny home from the hospital to die at home. The cancer had reduced her to little more than a skeleton, and the pain that had racked her body for two months and burned away her flesh until the skin became transparent gave her a famished, unearthly appearance. Occasionally she allowed herself to be given morphine to relieve the consuming fire, but she made everyone promise not to give her any when death was close. She said she wanted to experience it.

The hours dragged on, and Granny lay unconscious on her bed at home. Or so it appeared. Occasionally someone would say something to her: "We love you, Mama," or, "Your sister May called," or some such thing. But there wasn't a flicker of recognition on her face. As far as anyone could tell, she was comatose, except for her moans.

Half a day went by like this as the death watch continued, with someone always by her side.

Now it was Ben's watch at her bedside. "Granny, it's me," he said softly, leaning down close to her. He felt her pulse to make sure she was still alive. "Granny, I love you. I'm going to miss you. I love you, I love you so much," he said. Over and over he told her how much he loved her, but she didn't respond in any way. Then he saw the girl. He put his mouth next to her ear and said, "Granny, I think there's—I think there's someone here to see you. Open your eyes. Please, open your eyes. It's a girl. A spirit girl."

At the word "spirit" Granny opened her eyes. She scanned the room, then saw the ghost. Her mouth opened in amazement, then her face lit up with a smile. "Oh, how beautiful! How beautiful!" She spoke in little more than a whisper. "Yes, I'm coming," she said.

"Who is it, Granny?" said Ben. "Who is it?"

Her eyelids sagged shut, and the ecstasy vanished from her face. She sank back into a coma. Outside a mockingbird sang its heart out from the top of the magnolia tree. Ben did not call the family in quite yet. He listened to the bird and thought of the girl. Granny knew her, he was sure. But who could she be? Who was this Abby? What did she have to do with Granny? Her connection to Granny only Granny knew, and now Granny was gone. It was the most sacred experience he had ever had, too precious to share, even with his mother.

Death came a half hour later, with all the family gathered round. Granny's eyes opened and stared straight ahead. She somehow found the strength to reach out to something that no one else could see. Her arm dropped. She died with a mysterious, joyous look on her face.

Ben came back to the present and saw the body of the young man whose name was Alvaro being lifted onto a stretcher.

They drove along Interstate 40 toward Albuquerque. Husband and wife sat in the front seats, brother and sister in the back. For twenty minutes everyone sat in silence. Everyone was thinking of Alvaro—and death.

It was Maria who finally broke the silence. "Sam, I'm sorry." She reached over and touched his arm.

"So am I," said Sam, taking her hand and squeezing it briefly. "What fools we were."

"Yes, we were."

Ben saw his dad's eyes mist over, as they always did during rare moments of tenderness.

Then Sam said, "Maria, I don't think I've ever appreciated you so much as when you took over and waved down that car. I can't tell you how much that meant to me."

"That? It was nothing."

"Yes, it was." He took her hand again and gave it a lively squeeze. "And we'll run the air conditioner your way from now on."

"No, Sam, we'll do it your way."

"No, really, it's all right. I can do it my way when I'm alone."

"No, you have a point. We should be willing to make a small sacrifice for all those penguins."

"Stop it, you two!" Sarah burst out.

"I've got a solution," said Ben. "Here's a penny." He held it up. "Heads you win, Mom. Tails you lose, Dad."

"Whatever," said Sam.

"OK, Mom?"

"OK."

Ben flipped the coin, caught it, and flipped it over on top of his other hand. "Tails, you lose, Dad. Sorry."

"Hey, wait a minute. How'd that go?"

"Heads, Mom wins. Tails, you lose."

"Hey!"

"Sorry, Dad, you agreed!"

Everybody laughed, including Sam. "Where'd you come up with that baloney?"

"Payback time, Dad. Remember the mountain lion?"

"What *about* the mountain lion?" said Sarah.

"It's a guy thing," Ben said. "You wouldn't understand."

"Oh no? Try me, squirt!"

Chapter 9

THE GENTLEMAN SNAKE

"Oooooh, isn't he *big!* Land sakes, let me get a good look at you, Ben! Look at him, Griffin. He'll be as tall as you before you can shake a stick at him!" Great Aunt Nelda was famous for her endless cheer, crab omelets, and passion for the game of Scrabble. Some people, especially Maria, thought she came on too strong, but Ben loved her. And she adored him, had adored him ever since she first laid eyes on his tiny brown body and said, "How like a Marks he looks in spite of his color!" She had been widowed for twenty years, and Griffin was her fourteen-year-old grandson.

Nelda, Griffin, and half a dozen other relatives formed the welcoming committee for the Conovers. They had gotten the Point Clear house ready and prepared a meal of fried mullet and speckled trout straight from Mobile Bay, which lapped at the beach beyond the cattails and the white picket fence outside the front door.

A dozen people from five to seventy sat down at the long table on the back porch with the familiar yellow tablecloth. Iced tea, coleslaw, crab gumbo, sweet cornmeal bread, and peach cobbler made up the rest of the meal.

Ben faced the window. He saw a bright moon peep through pine needles. He felt lucky to have a second home like this. When the family drove down the long white clamshell driveway under the oaks, pines, magnolias, and dogwoods, some of which his dad planted long ago, he felt safe and happy.

"Griffin, show Ben what you have," said Nelda when the boys finished their cobbler.

Griffin led Ben to the screened porch that extended along the front of the house facing the bay and switched on the light. "She's not there!" Griffin said as he inspected the empty birdcage. "She must have squeezed through—the wires. Yeah. You bad girl!"

"What?" said Ben.

"Fifi. My flying squirrel. Close the door."

Ben closed the door they had just come through.

"She's got to be here somewhere."

"What do we do when we find her?"

"Leave that to me. She'll try to bite you. You have to wear gloves." Griffin put on some old gardening gloves.

"Is that her?" said Ben. "Up there, in the corner, next to the ceiling?"

"Fifi, you bad girl!" Griffin pulled up a chair and reached up.

Just as Griffin's hand was about to close around Fifi, she pushed off the screen and sailed clear across the room. She landed in a white wicker rocker with a cushion in it.

"Wow! Did you see that?" said Ben. "I want Dad to see this!"

Within a minute the whole family, all twelve, gathered in the porch and watched Fifi fly back and forth across the room. Sometimes she flew from one screen to another, sometimes from screen to chair or sofa, like a jet landing on an aircraft carrier. The last time she landed in Nelda's hair and bit her on her finger when Nelda, flailing her hands about and yapping like a puppy, tried to knock her off. Poor Fifi scrambled up the screen again while everybody except Aunt Squatsy, who ran to get a Band-Aid, laughed and squealed.

Finally Sam said, "Why don't we just leave her alone for the night?"

They agreed to do that, and Ben, whose room was next to the porch, heard Fifi slap against the screen from time to time as he drifted off to sleep in the warm bosom of his father's large Southern family.

Ben's Aunt Alice lived alone in deep woods thirty miles north of Point Clear. She was divorced, and her two children were off at college. She didn't hang around the rest of the Conover family. Her only close neighbor was a black woman named Hattie. Hattie lived with her eleven-year-old grandson, Horace, and two black labs.

Horace had grown up in the woods after his mother died when he was two. He knew where to pick wild huckleberries and where you could usually find a snake, turtle or 'possum. He had named the local deer and could imitate the delicate call of the whippoorwill and the human-like scream of the bobcat. He knew how to smoke out bees and take their wild honey without getting bitten. When the weather was warm, he bathed in the spring-fed waters of the creek that cut through the property and kept track of the dam-building activity of a family of beavers downstream. He once discovered a two-foot-long salamander in that creek, brought it home wriggling and put it in Hattie's biggest cooking pot, then fed it weenies until it finally died of indigestion. He had a lively imagination and loved adventure in any form. He played soccer and baseball in Bay Minette ten miles down the highway, but his first love was the woods.

It was about five o'clock when Ben and Horace decided to hike upstream from the swimming hole as far as they could go. Horace wanted to find the spring that the creek came from. He also wanted to make a good impression on the "kid from California."

"Back by seven, no later," Alice said. "And watch out for snakes!"

"Will they be safe?" Maria worried.

"Horace knows these woods like the back of his hand. Don't you, Sweetie?"

The boys splashed up the creek between banks two to three feet high. Often they climbed over or ducked under fallen trees. The creek narrowed, then widened; sometimes it twisted right and left, sometimes it straightened for a hundred yards or so. Sometimes the dense green foliage completely blocked out the sun, sometimes it let in a few stray rays. A woodpecker pecked away, frogs leaped into the water with a plop, cicadas droned on. Spiders draped their great webs across the creek, and the boys carried makeshift staffs to bat them aside. The afternoon was hot and dry; it hadn't rained in ten days, a long time for August in these parts.

"Look at that!" said Ben. Two armadillos hopped along the bank downstream. "They're fast. I never knew that."

"They're all around here," said Horace. "They'll come right up to you if you're still."

"I bet you've seen lots of flying squirrels."

"No. Only some dead baby ones. A hurricane knocked their nest out of a tree. They're all around here, but no one sees them. They only come out at night."

"I saw one today. My cousin *has* one."

"You're kidding!"

"No, he showed it to me. He carries it around in his shirt pocket. It looks like a chipmunk, except that it's gray."

"Cool!"

The boys splashed ahead; sometimes the creek came only up to their ankles, sometimes over their knees. The sandy bottom felt good on their feet, and the clear water sparkled as it gurgled over logs or eddied around fallen limbs.

They came to a thick-trunked magnolia leaning over the creek. "This is as far as I usually go," said Horace.

Ben checked his watch. It said 5:25. "We can go until six. That's at least a mile more. Do we have enough water?"

Horace jiggled the canteen. "Sure."

"Are we still on your property?"

"No. That was way back."

On they went. A school of minnows darted out of their way. A rabbit scurried into the brush as they advanced.

"Look!" said Ben. He stopped and pointed to a snake oozing out of a hole halfway up the bank. "What kind is it?"

"Just a water snake." Horace went up to it and grabbed it behind the head. "Here, you hold it. Behind the head, like this. It's not poisonous, but it can still bite."

"Looks like a copperhead to me," said Ben, whose knowledge of the local snakes was limited to books.

"Sort of. Here." Horace handed the snake over to the bigger boy.

Ben nervously took the snake and let it wrap its pink and brown three-foot-long body around his arm as he pinched it at the neck. "This is the first time I've held a snake," he said.

"I've held lots of them," Horace said.

Ben placed his arm next to the bank, and the snake wriggled off and made its escape. The boys continued upstream.

"I wonder when the last time somebody came this way," said Horace.

"It's like the Amazon," said Ben.

"Are you scared?" said Horace.

Ben was just a little. He had never seen thicker jungles even in the movies. He felt hemmed in, as if he were crawling through a beautiful but stifling green burrow. The low-hanging boughs dimmed the sunlight, and there was a strange quiet in the air—as if even the birds were afraid to venture so deep in the woods. He reminded himself he was in Alabama, not Africa or India or South America with its big cats or great snakes. "It's so dark. But it's only quarter to six," he said. "Do you want to turn around?"

Horace didn't answer, so the boys kept splashing forward.

Ahead they saw a fallen water oak which grew sideways out of the bank across the creek. Then they saw something else. They saw it at the same instant, and they both let out a yelp and jumped back. Ben turned and ran back a few steps. He felt the urge to keep running, to run by leaps and bounds all the way back down the creek to the swimming hole. But Horace froze in his tracks, then slowly stepped forward two, three paces, and halted about twenty feet from the tree.

It acted as if it hadn't seen them. It slithered along the tree across the creek, all nine feet of its massive diamond-backed body.

Ben stole up next to his brave little companion as the snake's head reached the other side. The tail with its great rattle passed in front of them.

"The gentleman snake!" said Horace in a hushed, reverent voice.

"We ought to go back," Ben said.

"No. Let's stay and watch. That's the biggest snake I ever saw outside of a zoo," said Horace, his voice still hushed, his whole body tense with excitement. "You're lucky. You'll never see a bigger snake, not in these woods. The Good Lord has blessed us."

"OK. But let's go back." There was something like terror in Ben's gut.

But Horace acted as if he hadn't heard Ben. With delicate steps he climbed up the low bank on the side opposite the snake, which was about 15 feet away, the width of the creek, and took a seat next to the tree trunk on the silty bank covered with leaves. Ben had little choice but to follow. He took his seat right next to Horace, but on the other side of the trunk. From their safe perch they watched while barely breathing at the great snake as it glided down the opposite bank to the water.

"Why do you call it the gentleman snake?" Ben said, his voice quivery, but his courage returning.

"Because you have to really bother a diamondback rattler before it strikes. And it gives lots of warning."

The boys watched as the snake drank. "It's huge, isn't it?" said Ben. His voice reflected his awe.

"As big as the python in the New Orleans zoo," said Horace, holding his hands wide apart.

"As big as the anaconda in the San Diego zoo!" said Ben, holding his hands even wider apart.

Both boys giggled nervously. "Shhh!" said Ben.

But the great gentleman snake did not look up. They might as well not have been there.

After a while Ben looked at his watch and said, "It's almost six." The snake lay languidly at the water's edge.

"Let's throw something at it and make it rattle," said Horace.

But before Ben could agree, the snake began to move again. Ever so slowly it raised itself, its diamond-shaped head with jaws full of death moving left then right, right then left, ahead of its skinny neck and gradually fattening body, as thick as Ben's thigh at the fattest point.

"He might come back this way," whispered Ben.

"He probably will," said Horace.

"What!"

"You go, I'm staying."

"You can't stay! It'll pass right next to you! Your knee's touching the tree!"

"He's a gentleman snake. I'll stay very still."

"He might crawl down in your lap."

"That'll be interesting."

The snake's head reached the far end of the tree and fulfilled Ben's greatest fear. It turned in their direction. Inch by inch it lifted its great brown length studded with yellow-bordered diamonds up onto the tree. "If you're staying, I'm staying too!" Ben whispered shrilly. "May God protect us."

"May God protect us," Horace repeated calmly. He took his eyes off the snake and looked at Ben, whose face reflected a war going on within. "And he will, if we don't move. *Don't move. Don't even breathe.*"

Both boys tried not to breathe and watched the slowly approaching snake. They saw its forked tongue dart out as its tail finally raised itself onto the tree. Suddenly Ben remembered that he, the oldest, was responsible for Horace. He felt a sweaty dread settle over him. He knew he should have grabbed Horace. Could he still do it? He was about to lunge at Horace when Horace whispered, "He's our friend. Look at him. He's beautiful!"

There was nothing to do but sit still as stone. Even to pray would have been a dangerous distraction. As for Abby, Ben never even wondered where she was, why she didn't show up at that moment. Being still, not shivering, not even breathing—this required total attention. Did he dare turn his head as the snake passed? Did he dare even blink? Just how much of a gentleman was this great snake with enough venom to finish off either one of them with a snap of its jaws?

Four feet away, the snake stopped, its tongue flitting out over and over, its head perfectly still. There was still time to jump back. And Ben would have at that instant if it weren't for Horace. But Ben knew that Horace was in the game for keeps. Just like he was when he climbed the pine in the howling wind. At that moment Ben would have given anything to be in that tree seventy feet above the California earth rather than staring down a rattler on the floor of an Alabama jungle.

What did the snake see sitting so close on both sides of its private highway? Didn't it notice that something was different, something out of the ordinary, something wrong? Wasn't it just a little worried about what might happen when it passed between those two living stumps? Didn't it know that men were its greatest enemy, that men almost always killed rattlers on sight? Or did it know something about these particular little men that told it they weren't a danger?

It jerked forward about an inch, then stopped, its tongue flitting in and out. Then on it came. It paused at Horace's knee and looked straight up into his face. Was murder in those jaws? Then it looked left and up at Ben, its fangs no more than six inches from Ben's leg. Ben stared back, not daring to blink, fighting back his fear, as the snake's tongue continued to go in and out. Then the snake looked ahead and lurched forward. The boys heard it pass between them with a soft scuffing sound that lasted forever, watched each diamond on its great back inch by out of vision until even the rattles on the snake's tail passed.

Then they saw nothing, heard nothing except a rustling to their rear and the rapid beating of their own hearts. They sat still for a few minutes. Then Ben whispered, "I'm going to turn round, turn my head around."

"OK," Horace whispered back.

Ben imagined the snake poised to strike just inches away when he decided at last to look behind him. Like the second hand on a clock, his head slowly turned. The shadows in the forest had deepened. Could he trust his own eyes? If only he could see the snake, see it way off out of striking distance. But he couldn't find it anywhere.

He decided to make his move. He sprang forward into the creek and landed with a splash on hands and knees. Right behind him came Horace, who crashed into him. They stood up dripping and looked back. They looked down at their feet and all around. They couldn't believe their good luck. There was no snake! But was it really gone? Didn't it lurk with murder on its mind behind that bush? "You and your gentleman snake," said Ben with a wild grin. "Let's get out of here!"

For the next minute they ran downstream like madmen. Only then did they feel safe. Only then did they stop to rest and drink their water.

"Were you scared?" said Ben.

"I *was* scared. Were *you* scared?" said Horace.

"I was so scared I peed in my pants. Just a little."

"You did? *Me too!*"

They looked into each other's eyes and laughed like crazy men whose death sentence had just been lifted.

A few days later Ben told his father about the huge snake. He was afraid of his dad's reaction, but he just couldn't keep it to himself any longer. He was willing to face the fierce scolding he knew he deserved.

They were sitting out at the end of the wharf and shelling crabs in the shade of the pavilion. It was hot, but a breeze blew across the bay out of the southwest. It was like every other day in late August. Hot, muggy, sweaty, but thank God for a breeze.

"How big was it really, Ben?"

"Huge. Almost as long as the boat." Ben looked over at the rowboat hanging by cables under the pavilion.

Sam just kept on staring at the crab he was working on. "What'd it do?"

"It was going down to the stream to get a drink of water."

"So you just sat and watched it? You didn't throw something at it to see what it would do? I sure would have. I'd want to hear it rattle."

"Horace almost did, but..." Ben hesitated. Should he describe what really happened?

"Yeah?"

"Well, the snake started to crawl back up before we – before we could."

"Yeah, then what?"

"You won't believe this. Don't be mad, OK?"

Sam stopped picking and looked up at his son. "What happened?"

"The snake passed right by us, just inches away. It looked straight at me, and I kept my cool. I'll never forget that look. But it didn't seem to mind us. It seemed to trust us."

"Yeah? What next?"

"What next? Well, it was over. We just jumped into the creek and ran like bloody murder back home. We were really scared! We were scared to death! But we were brave. I never would have done it on my own."

"So it was Horace who talked you into it?"

"He did. He said it was a gentleman snake. He said it warned you before it bit you. He knew it wouldn't bother us if we were still, so we didn't even blink. We didn't even *breathe*."

"You didn't?"

"It seemed like I didn't."

Sam began to laugh. He laughed and he laughed. And then Ben started to laugh.

When they calmed down, Sam said, "Wait till we get back to California before you tell your mother, OK?"

"One more secret. They never stop coming. You're not *mad?*"

"Why should I be?" Sam went back to picking at his crab. Then he looked up at his son. "Where was the girl in all this?"

"The girl? Oh, you mean—*her?*"

"I thought she might be there to protect you, you know, like a guardian angel. Isn't that what kept the snake from biting you?" He had a twinkle in his eye.

Ben knew his dad was making fun of him and didn't take the bait.

Sam paused. He seemed to be dredging up something deep within him. Finally he said, "That brings me back to that old Indian back in the desert. Did you really see him, or did you make it up to help the boy die? I've been meaning to talk to you about that."

"You mean Alvaro's grandfather?"

"Yeah, if that's what you want to call it."

"Sure, he was right there. Did *you* see him?"

Sam snorted. "Of course I didn't. Think back. Weren't you just helping—what was his name?"

"You mean Alvaro?"

"That's right. Weren't you just trying to help Alvaro die, die in peace? Think carefully. You made up the old Indian, right?"

"No, Dad. Alvaro saw him too. If I was making it up, how come Alvaro saw him?"

Sam looked out across the bay at five pelicans flying by in formation. The warm wind lifted what little hair was left on the top of his head. "You set him up, Ben. Maybe not consciously. You put the thought in Alvaro's mind. And it was just your imagination."

Ben listened to the slapping of the waves against the supports and shook his head.

"Something else I've been meaning to ask you. How come you saw that old Indian if you were taking your meds?" Sam looked straight into his son's soul with his piercing blue eyes.

Now it was Ben's turn to look out across the bay. When the air was clear, especially after a storm had come through, you could see Mobile way in the distance. The city was visible now, but it didn't register on Ben. All he could think of was how he had scammed his dad. "I—I—I didn't take the pills."

"You didn't take the pills? Why not?" Sam's voice was surprisingly calm.

"They made me sick. I—flushed them down the toilet."

Ben held his breath.

Sam just stared at his son.

"If I'd taken them, I wouldn't have been able to help Alvaro."

Without a word Sam dropped the crab he had been working on, brushed his hand off against each other, and stood up and walked down the wharf toward the house.

Chapter 10

THE DYBBUK

The afternoon wind huffed out of the southwest, the waves splashed against the uprights, and the old wharf groaned. Maria in her black one-piece bathing suit sat reading a magazine in a wooden chair under the pavilion. Sam fished for speckled trout with his rod and reel, and Ben threw the fishing net. Nelda and the Jewish woman in her eighties named Gretl who lived next door played Scrabble on a card table that Sam had carried out.

The bay teemed with life. Brown pelicans, their big gawky bills tucked in with self-importance, perched on every post sticking up out of the water. Others flew about and splashed into the water in search of dinner. Far out in the bay porpoises swam in single file, their fins rising and falling in a lazy arc. Seagulls squealed overhead, and a blue heron landed on the next wharf with a screech. A few fishing skiffs out in the bay dipped and rose, and a speedboat droned and banged its way across the choppy surface.

"Look at these beauties!" Ben held up his net. Half a dozen shrimp and a flapping mullet more than a foot long were the prize.

"Good for you!" said Maria.

"You're having more luck than me," said Sam.

"Maybe I'm a better fisherman."

Sam didn't quite manage a smile.

Suddenly the sound of a man shouting profanities made its way upwind from the beach to the pavilion.

"What in the world…?" said Maria.

"It's *him!*" said Gretl. "It's *him!*"

The profanity spewed out of the man's mouth without letup. He seemed to be shouting at someone right in front of him as he walked along, bending first under one wharf where it met the beach, then the next. He spoke in a loud, blasting voice that cut through the wind.

"Who is he?" said Sam, who had just come up to the women.

"I don't know," said Gretl. "He comes this way about once every month or so. He'll go up the beach quite a way, then come back."

"What's wrong with him?" said Ben.

"You'd laugh if I told you what I think, child."

"He's probably off his medication," said Sam.

"I once saw a man like him in Mexico when I was a girl," said Maria. "In my grandfather's village. They said he was possessed by a demon."

A demon. Something inside Ben snapped to attention. Behind him the mullet flopped around in the net lying across the sun-bleached wharf, forgotten.

"A dybbuk, to be more exact, that's what I'd say," said Gretl.

"A what?" said Nelda.

"A dybbuk. A tramp soul. It's taken over the man's body."

Ben watched with fascination as the man walked rigidly forward, his arms barely moving, the filth pouring out of his mouth nonstop.

The pleasant spell of the afternoon had been broken, and the family took refuge in the house with its air-conditioning. Ben was excited, though, and he wouldn't stop asking Gretl questions.

"But where does a dybbuk come from, Aunt Gretl?"

"From the world beyond. The world we'll all go to when we die."

"How could he leave that world if he's dead?" Ben wasn't thinking only of the dybbuk. He was thinking of the girl, Uncle Dan, his grandmother, and the people who walked the mall. Maybe Gretl knew something. He was all ears.

"He must have been very unhappy there. Maybe he was bored. Or maybe he hated the Lord and wanted to get away. Maybe he was *thrown* out for all I know." Gretl threw up her tiny, shriveled hands. "I'm not a rabbi!"

"He's psychotic, and he's off his medication," said Sam.

"Oh, but a dybbuk's so much more exciting," drawled Nelda. "I'd like to think it's a dybbuk, wouldn't you, Ben?"

Ben flashed a nervous smile at Nelda, then looked back at his dad and scowled.

Sam hesitated before he spoke, then said, "If mentally ill people stay on their medication, they stay calm and can function. If they don't, they go insane. And millions of depressed people are on Prozac. It takes away their depression. Where Gretl sees a dybbuk, I see a sick brain."

There was a lull in the conversation until Gretl said, "Maybe dybbuks don't *like* medication. Maybe it makes them uncomfortable and they leave. And that's why the craziness goes away."

"Mom took Prozac for a while," said Ben.

"Ben!" said Sam sternly.

"What? I'm sorry. I didn't know — that — "

"That's all right," said Maria. "Yes, I did for a while, and it helped."

Ben couldn't resist asking the next logical question. "Aunt Gretl, are you saying that Mom had a dybbuk in her?"

"No, of course not," Gretl snapped back. "But that man— that's a different story."

"I say it's a dybbuk!" said Nelda in her Southern drawl as she carried out a tray of iced tea to the dining room table where they sat. "Let's put it to a vote, what do you say? How many say he's off his medication?"

Sam's hand went up. Maria's jerked up halfway, then settled back down, then went back up.

"How many say it's a dybbuk?" Nelda said.

Nelda put down the tray and held her hand high, followed by Gretl.

"Well, Sugar," she said, looking at Ben, "it looks like it's up to you. Which is it?"

Ben looked at each of his elders. They looked at him as if he were a judge about to render an important verdict. "I'll let you know in a little bit," he said.

Ben lay in the hammock on the screen porch and waited. He knew the cursing man would be coming back, and he strained to hear the voice through the wind as it rustled through the oaks and lifted the Spanish moss hanging from branches like fleecy beards. There it was! It pierced the breeze like a bolt of lightning. Ben skipped out the screen door down the brick walkway and turned right along the shady boardwalk that led to the hotel a mile up the beach. He climbed onto a low magnolia branch that extended low over the path. Hidden and out of danger, he could decide what to do. He didn't know exactly what he was up against, but a voice inside him—was it Granny?—told him he had business with it. He knew everybody would be shocked to know what he planned to do. He was glad they were three houses away.

As the man approached, Ben waited and watched. The man was of average size, probably around thirty, and walked looking straight ahead, as if in a trance. His thrust-out chest gave him an athletic look, but his rigid shoulders and swingless arms made him resemble a mechanical toy soldier. He wore a drab tee shirt and shorts.

The cursing blasted out of his mouth without a pause. But it wasn't what the man said that Ben paid special attention to; it was the way it sounded. The words boomed out as if they were spoken through a megaphone, and the quality of the voice was unnatural. It was as if the man's vocal chords were made of metal. They had a weird, deep twang.

The man seethed with hatred as he spoke. Each word was a missile intended to hurt. No, that wasn't exactly it. As Ben concentrated, he began to feel the man's pain. The man was avenging himself on someone.

No, that wasn't it either. Something was very strange. Ben suddenly felt that the man he saw wasn't who he seemed to be. He thought back to Dingo. It was like that. Yes, it was like that. There seemed to be two beings inside the one body. Ben thought of Gretl's dybbuk, and his scalp tingled. A tremendous surge of excitement mixed with fear shot through him. But he wasn't as afraid as he would have been if he hadn't met it before. Ben decided to confront the unseen thing inside the man's body.

Ben jumped off the limb onto the path. The man stopped about ten feet away and held his hands in front of his chest. He clawed at his chest with his fingernails, and the cursing stopped. For a moment his head hung down, and his eyes stared out of the top of their sockets just below the eyebrows.

Then like a whip the man threw back his head and fixed his hating eyes on Ben. With a great roar he began to curse again, but now at Ben. He lunged toward Ben, but Ben darted back in plenty of time and screamed, "Stop it!" The man seemed stunned. His head rolled around on his neck, and he began to stagger around, as if drunk, but with his eyes fixed on Ben in an alarmed stare. Mixed in with the profanity were roars.

Ben, with heart racing, held up his hands and approached the man. "Come out of him, dybbuk!" he said forcefully and as loudly as he could. "Go back to your own world!"

With a roar that could be heard by fishermen out in the bay, the man lunged at Ben again. But Ben, like a matador, stepped aside. "Come out of him, dybbuk!"

This time the man did not lunge, but instead began slowly backing up under Ben's intense stare. "Come out of him!" Ben repeated, made bold by his own seeming power.

Then the strangest thing happened. The man, with feet wide apart, bent from the waist and began swinging the upper half of his body in a circle. Faster and faster the man's torso spun until he almost resembled an airplane propeller. The man's long hair whipped violently back and forth, and foam from his mouth flew about wildly. His face was horribly contorted. The whole effect was uncanny, unnatural and frightening, but Ben mastered his fear. He had a grip on whatever it was, and he wasn't about to let go. Finally the man stopped his gyrations. He breathed in jagged snores, his face blotched with spit.

"Come out of him. Come OUT of him, dybbuk!" Ben screamed.

"Who are you?" said the man in his metallic voice, his eyes

staring out of the side of his face at Ben. "You can't tell me what to do. You want to fight me? I'll show you!"

The man then turned his head back toward Ben and spat, but Ben held his ground. "Come out of him in the name of all that is good!" he yelled. "Come out of him in the name of all that is good!" Ben kept repeating these words.

The man began shaking, twisting and moaning. He seemed to be in terrible pain. Then he looked up at the sky, threw up his arms, and fell to the ground, shaking and whimpering.

Gradually he quieted. The hate that had distorted his face disappeared. His whole body looked relaxed. Ben could hardly believe it. Ever so cautiously, he crept closer to the man. Right next him, but ready to spring back, he repeated the command to come out. But it wasn't necessary. The man, or whatever was in him, had given up the fight.

Ben stooped down and tenderly put his hand on the man's head. The man did not resist, and Ben took off his shirt and wiped the man's forehead. An old couple, who had been watching from the back porch of the nearest house, walked up.

"Where am I?" said the man suddenly as he sat up. "Who are you?" His voice was normal. The tinny sound was gone.

"I'm a kid who lives down the beach. Can you get home—by yourself?"

The man looked around and tried to get his bearing.

"My dad'll give you a ride home."

"Okay," said the man as Ben took his arm and steadied him. There was no hint of the beast that raved a few moments before.

"Who *is* that kid?" said the old woman to her husband, standing by their gate so close by that Ben overheard her.

"He's visiting the Conovers. They say he's from California."

"Oh, that explains it! You know what I'm going to do? I'm going to call Nelda and tell her exactly what we saw." She took a last look at Ben still holding the man's arm as they made their way down the path under the oaks. Then she turned and went into her house.

The first thing Sam did when he and Ben dropped off the man was ask the receptionist about the man's medications.

"Sometimes he gets off them," she admitted, "and then he starts cussing and takes off. It's horrible. It's sickening. The police won't do anything about it. So I wait till he comes back, and we trick him into taking his meds. Then he's fine. But how come he's all right now? He's never come back this way before. Did you give him something?"

"Not a thing. My son here—did something to him."

"It just goes to prove my point," said Gretl when Sam and Ben got back. "This boy of yours has power over dybbuks. I can feel it in him."

"Oh, come on, Gretl," said Sam, "why do the drugs work? It's just a chemical imbalance. The medicine restores the chemistry. That's all."

"How did *Ben* restore the chemistry, Mr. Smarty Pants?" said Gretl with a bright-eyed, sassy smile as full of wrinkles as a prune.

Sam's brow knit. "That I can't say."

"I can! The medicine chases the dybbuk away. And so did Ben. It's like throwing tear gas into a room. People clear out." Then she turned her thin bespectacled face at Ben and asked, "What do *you* say? What did it actually feel like, child? Tell me as exactly as you can. I want to know."

Ben swallowed a mouthful of watermelon and said, "There was something inside that man, but it wasn't him. That's what it felt like."

"Didn't I tell you!" cried Gretl triumphantly. "That's a dybbuk for you!"

"You have to know Ben better," said Sam. "He's got a terrific imagination."

"I'd *love* to get to know Ben better!" Gretl beamed at him as if he were the only person in the world who understood her.

"What I'd like to know, Ben," said Sam, "is how you *did* it."

"I told it to come out of him in the name of all that's good, that's all. Really."

The adults studied Ben for a moment. All they could see was a normal looking twelve-year-old boy.

"Where is Nelda anyway?" said Gretl. "She promised me another game of Scrabble."

"Can I play, too?" said Ben.

"Of course, you can. But you'll find your Aunt Gretl tougher to beat than some old dybbuk."

"Gretl, how do you spell *dybbuk*?"

Gretl's eyes lit up with delight. "I'll tell you when the game's over, child! I'll tell you when the game's over!" Then she leaned back in her chair and cackled.

Chapter 11

THE MASTERPIECE

Every morning except Sundays Sam and Ben did yard work. They usually started about nine and worked for an hour, but sometimes they went past noon. Their tools included three different kinds of clippers, a saw, a machete, a pick, a ladder, and work gloves. Their main task was to clear away the vines and creepers that were choking the shrubs and trees on the property. When they finished the morning's sweaty work, they looked like drowned moles. Maria made them dip in the bay before coming in to shower. It was gruelling work, nothing even close to fun, but Ben understood its purpose and didn't complain.

One day Ben and Sam worked together pulling wild wisteria from a young magnolia in the side yard. "This stuff's like the graffiti that gets scribbled all over our cities," said Sam as they worked. "As soon as you get rid of it, it comes right back. LET GO, YOU BEAST!" he yelled at the vine as they tugged together. It finally did, and both tumbled backward on their bottoms. They were too angry at the vine to laugh even. Then Ben felt an idea taking shape in his mind. He thought it through for a while as they continued to cut and pull. Should he do it?

"Dad, didn't I see some paint in the tool shed?"

"Some spray paint, yeah."

"Yeah, different colors."

"That's right." Sam was so absorbed in the next vine that he didn't bother to ask Ben what he had in mind. Ben was glad of that.

There was a knock at the back door, then a second, louder knock.

"What in the world...?" said Sam as he rolled out of bed.

"What could that be?" said Maria.

The big red numbers on the electric clock said 5:03. There wasn't enough light outside to see who it was. What Sam saw were the silhouettes of a big man and a boy about the size of Ben.

"Who is it?" said Sam as he switched on the outside light.

"It's Deputy Sheriff Calvin. Are you this boy's father?"

"Ben. What are you...? Are you all right? ...What's going on, Sheriff?"

"I caught this boy spraying graffiti on private property just up the road."

"*What?*"

"What is it, Sam?" said Maria from the shadows behind.

"I'm going to release him into your custody on condition that you bring him to the juvenile detention center later this morning. That's in Bay Minette. Do you agree to do that?"

"Yes, I do," said Sam, still not believing his ears.

"Ben, is that you?" Maria cried out.

"Yeah, Honey," said Sam. "It's a... He's OK. I'll explain it in a minute."

"I usually bring 'em in," said the Deputy, "but he seemed like a nice boy, and I got permission to come by here. He says it's a first offense. If that's so, they should go easy on him."

Deeply ashamed, Sam looked at Ben, then back at the deputy. "What do you mean by 'easy'?"

"Oh, restitution and community service. Something like

that. Actually we don't often get graffiti around here. Don't sound like y'all from around here."

"No, we're from…uh…did you say the juvenile detention center?"

"Yeah, they'll be expecting him later this morning. Oh, and I have to keep these spray cans as evidence."

Sam stared at the cans. He recognized them as the cans in the tool shed. "Thanks, Deputy. And I'm sorry about this."

"Sorry to disturb you." Then he looked at Ben and said, "Keep out of trouble from now on, boy, you hear?"

"What's going on?" called Sarah from the door of her bedroom.

"Ben got caught spraying graffiti on a building," said Sam in a low voice.

"What'd you say?"

"He got caught *tagging!*" Sam growled as he glowered at Ben.

"Whaaat? Ben!?" She brought her hand to her mouth.

Ben had blue spray on his shirt. Sam said, "Go out on the end of the wharf. No, first change your shirt. Then go out there and wait. I'll be right behind you. Now go!"

All Ben could think of as he changed his shirt was the suppressed rage in his father's voice. For a moment he wished he had never been born.

When Sam joined Ben under the pavilion, the sky across the bay was pink, and Ben saw a belt in his father's hand.

"I'm sorry," Ben said as he got into the car.

For a moment Sam didn't say anything. The car crunched its way down the clamshell driveway.

"Dad, I…I…" Then he put his hand over his eyes like a

visor and looked down at his lap.

Sam was in no mood to comfort him. Instead he said, "If someone told me there was a hole in the bay, and all the water had been sucked into it, I would have believed them sooner than this. You're lucky I didn't beat you with that belt, like my dad did to me more than once."

They turned right out of the driveway onto Scenic Highway 98 and headed south as a dull pink lit up the east.

"We talked about graffiti when we worked in the yard the other day. Do you remember?" Sam's voice quivered with disappointment. "Community service. Do you know what that means? You might not get home in time for school. And I've got a job in two weeks. How in the world could you have done this? What in God's name came over you? You of all people!"

Ben said nothing, and Sam went on: "You know what? After you healed that man, I began to wonder if you had—well, some kind of special gift. But it turns out you're just a punk, a vandal, like a million other kids in this godforsaken world. I'm embarrassed! I'm mortified! I'm horrified at what you did! And I want you to know it! If you ever do anything like this again, if you inflict this kind of suffering on your mother ever again, I'll use the belt on you. Do you understand? …Where is this masterpiece you painted?" he said after a bit. "I want to see it! I want you to see it too by the light of day! Where is it?"

"Turn around," Ben said faintly.

Sam braked hard and turned the car into a driveway. Then he squealed up the road.

"The next right," Ben said.

They turned up a farm road.

"It's right there," Ben said.

He pointed to a ramshackle hamburger stand that had been condemned and deserted for at least three years. The headlights shone directly on it, and Sam saw graffiti painted on it—and something else. He clicked on the brights.

They both got out and walked up closer. Next to the graffiti was a picture, a picture of a girl.

"What the hell?!" said Sam.

"That's Abby. That's what she looks like, sort of. There was a moon, but it was still pretty dark."

Then Sam read words painted on the plywood that boarded up the stand: "Abby, I will love you forever."

Sam blinked in disbelief, then looked down at his son, who held a hand over his eyes with head bowed. Sam's eyes filled with tears, and Ben looked up and saw them glistening in the dawn. But he couldn't guess what those tears meant.

"Why did you do it?" Now there was no hint of anger in Sam's voice. There was only amazement.

Ben did not answer right away. He listened to the steady drone of a hundred crickets and felt with his bare feet the dewy grass growing between cracks in the dilapidated asphalt parking lot. Then he looked up at his father and said, "It was my declaration of love. That's all. Stupid, wasn't it?"

Sam and Ben stood in silence side by side. They stood that way, father and son, for over a minute, and Ben heard his father sob violently one time, then check himself.

Nothing stirred in the warm gray dawn as they stared at Ben's masterpiece except two cardinals, which flitted and chirped in a nearby azalea bush.

Later that morning Ben told the officer in charge at an informal private hearing what he painted. The officer listened respectfully, then said, "So you have a girlfriend named Abby?"

"Yes, Sir."

"It says here you're not from these parts. The Deputy said your car has California plates. Is that right?" Now he looked at Sam.

"Yes, Sir."

"Ya'll from California?"

"Yes, Sir."

He turned back to Ben. "Is that the sort of stuff they paint back in California?"

"No, Sir."

"It says here you even painted her picture."

"As best I could, yes, sir. But it was kind of dark."

"Why'd you do it?"

"I—uh—I don't know. I guess I thought it was nice. She's pretty, and I can draw pretty good. And I do love her. I love her a lot."

For a few moments the officer stared at Ben as a blue jay squawked outside the building. Finally he said, "It's your first offense?"

"Yes, Sir."

"How'd you like to paint the front of that building a nice glossy white?"

"I'd like that, Sir. I'd like that a lot."

"Mr. Conover, see to it that young Ben here does just that."

"Yes, Sir. I will."

"And do it today if it don't storm," said the officer, looking out the window, then back at Ben. "If it were up to me, I'd ask you to leave it there and put you in for a county beautification award."

Ben's face lit up with surprise.

The officer looked at Sam and said, "Don't worry, Mr. Conover, I'll see to it that it don't go on his record." Then he said with a wry smile, while looking at Ben, "I guess if you got to break the law, you might as well do it with style. Kid, you're one of a kind."

Chapter 12

THE BOMBSHELL

On a sultry mid-August afternoon, Sam Conover had a message for his son. They had biked a mile up the boardwalk to the Grand Hotel and watched a man in a sailor's uniform fire a polished bronze cannon mounted on giant spoked wheels pointing out over the Bay, a relic from Civil War days. That's what happened every day at 4 pm. It was a ritual memorializing the hotel's rich military history.

"During the Civil War the hotel served as a hospital for wounded Confederate soldiers," Sam said after the cluster of spectators broke up. "Over three hundred died and are buried on these grounds in a common unmarked grave. Then in World War Two it was used as a training school by the Army Air force. Over five thousand soldiers learned basic seamanship here."

"Interesting," said Ben as he wiped the sweat off his nose.

"To a Marine like me it's more than interesting. Just thinking about this history makes me tingle all over."

"I can understand that," said Ben.

"Actually I don't think you can. And that's why I've brought you here."

They walked their bikes back to the interior of the property with its ancient live oaks, flowers, and fountains, and found a wrought-iron bench under one of the oaks. Not far away kids' feet were sticking up out of a hammock. A honeymooning couple strolled by in front of them.

"Nice, eh?" Sam said.

"Yeah, beautiful."

They sat quietly for a minute, and Ben sensed that something unusual was about to be said. His dad seemed strangely serious, and the silence was getting a little scary. Then the bombshell hit.

"Son, I've decided to send you to a military academy this year."

Ben heard these words in disbelief. No, it was more like horror. "What? What are you saying? A military academy? You're kidding. Dad, you've got to be kidding."

"No, I'm not. It's a military academy located in South Carolina."

"What!? No way, Dad! No way. I've got—I've got basketball. Coach Jackson would die if I didn't show up. I owe it to him. And my friends. And Mom, and—and you. No way. Why? Why?"

"Because I love you enough to cough up twenty-five thousand dollars to send you there. That's why. It's a boarding school."

"A boarding school? A boarding school? But why?"

"Because you need a completely different environment. It provides structure, organization, self-discipline. You wear a uniform. There's physical training every morning. They have a junior ROTC program. It's not the sort of place where kids, young men—uh, talk to ghosts."

"So that's it. Oh, now I get it. Dad, that's crazy. That's fine for some people, but it's not me. Don't ask me to march in formation. Don't ask me to wear a uniform. I'm not the drilling sort. I'd die in a place like that!"

"They have small classes, you get personal attention. It's a college prep school, not a reform school. You'd get used to it. And you'd shine. You always do."

"No, Dad. I'd suffocate. I'd go crazy. They'd end up kicking my ass out, and you'd lose all that money. No, Dad. I'm not going there!"

"You *are* going there. You need to be there in a week, and we're going to drive up there to get you situated. You won't be going back with us to California. We'll send everything you need. And by the way, they have a good basketball team. They are heavy into sports."

"No, Dad. What does Mom say about this?" By now Ben was close to sobbing. But he hadn't given up the fight. "I can't believe Mom would go along with this."

"I'll deal with your mother. Ben, let me emphasize. What you did to that shack is not normal. Seeing and talking to ghosts is not normal. It's, it's unnatural. You're my responsibility. I can't stand by and do nothing. I'm your father. Believe me, I wish I didn't have to do this. But it's for your own good."

"No, Dad, it's not for my own good. Do you think I'd care about basketball if you and Mom weren't there to watch me play? I can't believe this. I can't believe you're serious. Going to South Carolina isn't going to make Abby disappear. Dad, look, don't you think you're rushing into this? Look, let's make a deal. Look, I know how to shut out the spirits. Suppose I agree to shut them out. Suppose…"

"Would that include the girl?"

"Oh God! Dad, I love Abby. I love her. Don't ask me to shut her out. Just all the rest. And remember. The psychologist said I wasn't crazy. I'm just—different."

"No, Ben, he was being kind. You're just not quite right in the head. Not crazy. But, well, more than different. I'm worried about what it's leading to. I mean, a painting on a shack in the middle of the night? Does that really sound sane to you?"

"Look, Dad, okay, I'll do my best to shut Abby out."

"No, you *will* shut her out!"

"Okay, okay, but if I do, will you drop this crazy idea of going to South Carolina?"

For a moment there was quiet, just the rustle of leaves in the tree overhead. Ben sat and waited in horrified silence.

"All right, I'll think about it," his dad finally said. "But if you slip up, you'll spend seventh and eighth grade there, that I can guarantee. And maybe longer. If you slip up, you won't be graduating from Bakersfield High, but from Camden Military Academy."

Ben took a deep breath. He could hardly believe he was sitting in one of the most beautiful spots in the Deep South. According to his father it was at this spot in 1864 that the Confederacy sank the famous Union battleship *Tecumseh*, and that's what he found himself thinking about. He had taken a direct hit, a cannonball to the heart. He felt like he was in some kind of time warp, as if what his father told him was a weird and horrible fantasy. No Abby? It was unthinkable. Had he really given his word? Would it count as a lie if he secretly talked to her? In this beautiful place hell had opened its doors and given him a glimpse inside.

"Let's go back home," said his father.

In torment Ben got up on his bike. His father patted him on the back as they started out. A blue heron flying overhead screeched.

Chapter 13

THE VISIT

Ben loved to go out on the end of the wharf at night just before bed and listen to the waves softly slap against the posts. What was it about this place that made it so special? Dad would come out and fish for hours, and Mom would talk or text to her friends or pry crabs out of the trap and put them in a bucket for gumbo that night. Sometimes she'd even tell him where to throw the line! And Dad just took it in stride. Often they'd just quietly be together, aware of what the other was doing but thinking their own thoughts. Ben couldn't recall a single argument between them on the wharf. It was holy ground, a family refuge, a magnet for the best of times.

His father had relented, and South Carolina, with a lot of help from Maria and even from Sarah, was out of the picture at least for a while. On this particular night, the last before the long trip home, the sky was clear and the stars were blazing. Ben almost forgot that his father worried about his sanity and that his friends would be waiting for him with their taunts and "Ghost Boy" jokes when he got back home. They thought he was a little crazy too. If only they could meet, if only they could *see* Abby.

On other nights like this he had felt her presence but not seen her. On this night he felt her near again. "Ben," he heard. Or thought he heard. He listened hard but could only make out the faint sound of a whippoorwill in the distance.

"Ben." She suddenly whooshed into view and sat on

the bench opposite him. She glowed and was easily visible. Her light brown naturally curly hair hung down over her shoulders, and her eyes looked warm and sweet, but sad. She was fully present, her whole body, and she wore a simple dress that flowed out over her knees. Was it yellow, the color of the light that surrounded her? He couldn't tell. It was the first time he'd seen all of her since the day of the party three months before.

"Abby!" he said. He was too stunned to say more except again, "Abby!"

"I'm here. And it wasn't easy."

There was quiet; then he said the first thing that came to his mind: "Did you see my drawing? And the—and the note?"

"Yes. And the trouble you got into."

"And do you know I'm not supposed to be talking to you? That I told my dad I wouldn't? Do you know about South Carolina? My God, you're so beautiful! Are you my guardian angel or something?"

"I do know about South Carolina. My mentors are helping me. Helping me to help you. I don't know what they're planning yet. No, I'm not your guardian angel. I'm much too young. Granny is going to be your spirit guide. It takes special training. And stamina. And self-sacrifice."

"Oh… Then who are you? And why do you look after me? And why do I love you so much? And why do I feel like I've known you forever when I don't even know if—if you're real?"

"Real? Ben, how can you doubt that?"

"I don't. Not really. Not when you're right in front of me. But everybody tells me you're not, except my mom. They think you're a hallucination. And they make me wonder if

I'm crazy. It's very confusing, and sometimes I doubt myself."

"They're lots of kids like you, Ben. Plenty of them see spirits. *I'm* the one who's unusual. I have my own life where I live, but I want to be with you too much. My teachers discourage contact. You wrote that you love me. But I'm the one who loves. I love too much. And I'm not even in your world."

"You do love me?"

"Oh, if only you knew!"

"You do? But why? Why do you love me? You don't even know me…do you?"

"I'm an orphan."

"An orphan?" He was completely confused. "An orphan? Then your mom and dad are dead too?"

"No, you silly!" She smiled and chuckled. She was breathtakingly cute. "I'm an orphan because *I* died. My parents are back on earth."

"Oh." He had to think about that. Then he said, "Do you know who they are?"

"Of course I do. And I miss them. And I miss the life that should have been mine."

"Do you visit them like you visit me?"

"No. Except my mother. Once a year, earth time. On the Day of the Dead."

"That's just like my mom!"

"Ben, I love your mom, and I love your dad."

"You do? Why?"

"Because they're *my* mom and mad too!"

He was stunned. He didn't know what to say next. It was another of those moments like at the Grand Hotel. An unbelievable announcement from out of the blue. A time-stopper. Except that this time it lacked horror. It was just amazing, incomprehensible. "What—what do you mean?" he finally stammered.

"My teachers didn't want me to tell you this. They thought it might tie us together even more. But they didn't forbid it. They weren't sure. So here I am. And I'm telling you that we have the same mom and dad. And I want you to be sure to tell them this, but not yet. Once you do, they'll know I'm real. Even your dad."

"Abby, how can they be your mom and dad? What are you saying? Maybe I'm crazy after all. Maybe I'm imagining this!"

"You're not crazy, Ben. You're lucky. You're blessed. You see, I was your twin. You lived, and I died. I was dead at birth."

"NO! This can't be true. What are you saying? Who *are* you?!"

"It is true, and when you tell your dad how you found this out, he'll have to believe you. You can't tell him yet. But when you do, he'll believe in your gift, he'll know you're not crazy. He'll believe in me too, he'll know that I'm alive and love him, and it will give him great joy. They've been keeping this from you all these years."

"Abby, this is too much. You've got to be kidding. Why— why would they do that?"

"I don't understand earth people. Because it was too painful? Or maybe because they were ashamed? Earth people are strange. I don't know why. I just know they've been keeping this secret from you all these years."

"But that means you're my sister. No wonder I feel so close to you!"

"More than that, your *twin* sister. Yes, we spent a whole lot of time together. Inside Mom's tummy!"

"I don't believe this!" He blinked his eyes, came back to the sounds of the water plopping against the posts. Would she be there when he opened them? He opened them, and there she was, shining as before.

"Ben, my teachers are very interested in us. They want us to be happy. They say we should separate. One world at a time is enough, they say. When you got in trouble with the law, they counseled me right away. And when your father threatened to send you to that military school, that was it. "It's gone on long enough, it's gone too far," they said.

"Well, I don't think it has. I don't think it ever will. I think they're wrong!"

"The two worlds are meant to be apart. That's what they say. How will you ever have a real girlfriend if you're stuck on me? Don't you see?"

"I don't care. If you are my twin sister, why shouldn't I want to be with you?"

"You will be. And this is the other reason I've come to you. My teachers tell me that sooner or later I'll get another chance at life on earth. They say that earth is an experience not to be missed. I missed my chance. I'll get another. Ben"—now she spoke with great seriousness, as if she had reached a sacred moment in their conversation—"I want to come back as your daughter—they say that's possible. If that happens, we'll have *plenty* of time to be together."

"What? But this—this will mean—that's wonderful! But—"

"Do you see now why my guides worried I would tell you too much? Now you might feel you'll have to marry, and you might not want to. Or you'll marry too soon."

"Oh, but I will, if that means—"

"You can't know that. And there are other ways I can get

back to earth. Less ideal, but..."

"No, no, Abby, there is only one way. I'll be your dad. Oh, this is too awesome!"

"This is what they want me to leave you with. You can't tell your parents about any of this for an earth year. Wait until your next birthday, they say. My teachers hope your mom and dad—*our* mom and dad—will break the news to you so you won't have to break it to them. Better if they tell you than if you tell them. And they might. They've been tempted to many times. My teachers also hope you'll get more involved in the affairs of earth. 'One world at a time,' they keep saying. That applies to both of us."

"Does that mean I can't see you anymore? Is that what they're saying? That sucks."

"If you do, it'll be because I weaken. And I might. I'm happy where I am. I'm well cared for and loved. When your— our—Granny died, she found me almost as soon as she got here. And she is nothing but love. Amazing! But I know how I'll miss you. We have something like your Valentine's Day over here, and you were my valentine. Cross-world valentines are very rare. But I won't be visiting you. Not like this. Not talking to you."

"That hurts, Abby. That really hurts."

"It hurts me too, Ben. Heaven would be better with a taste of earth every now and then. Believe me, I'll be tempted to look in, even if I can't, you know, visit."

"But how will I ever convince Dad of all this? That you are his dead daughter? It's impossible enough for him to believe you're real! But a dead daughter?!"

"I have no idea. That's what my mentors are working on. I don't know yet, and it does worry me. Not just for your sake, but for mine too. We just have to be patient."

Ben noticed a sadness cross her face, and the aura surrounding her body flickered.

"Oh, I almost forgot," she said. "They say that what you did for Pam Grady was great—the girl at the party. No, *commendable* they said. They hope you'll do more of that. Sticking up for the underdog builds character, they say… I've got to go. I've got to go, Ben. I love you. I'm fading. I—I—"

"Don't leave me like this, Abby."

"It's not easy for me, either. But I'm giving out of energy, losing control. I'm—" Suddenly her shape disappeared, and where she had been, there was a beautiful blue circle, an orb, pulsing with love. Then it faded away.

Chapter 14

DUVALL

Ben took to heart what Abby told him. He made up his mind to throw himself into the affairs of earth and try to forget about—not Abby, he could never do that—but Abby's visits. He would try to adopt the philosophy of "one world at a time." At least that would make his dad happy and keep the military school at a distance. He decided to try out for the varsity basketball team composed of 8th graders. It might be a long shot, but if he didn't make it he could always drop back to the junior varsity team composed of 7th graders. Making that team would be a cinch.

Junior high turned out to be one world too many all by itself. Well, almost. Sure enough, Jared's reckless announcement was making the rounds, and people were constantly asking him about ghosts. Not usually out of meanness, but real curiosity. But there were the mean ones too, and "Ghost Boy" rang into his ears at almost every lunch hour. Sometimes he just smiled, but inside it hurt.

There was one kid who was the devil himself as far as Ben was concerned. This kid, Duvall Odom, wouldn't let up.

Ben and Duvall got acquainted in the strangest of ways.

On a day in early September just three weeks into the school year, Ben stood in a group of boys on the playground. Kids were still trying to discover who was cool to hang out with and who wasn't. All races were represented; there was some mingling, but for the most part the racial groups clustered together. Pretty much the sexes also kept to themselves; even girlfriends and boyfriends would usually meet after school, not during. The school dress code had been recently loosened, so pretty much anything you wore was acceptable. But the real dress code was something the school authorities had nothing to do with. Only a geek or a nerd would wear a shirt with buttons up the front or one that was brightly colored or plaid or was tucked in or that wasn't one or two sizes too big. Most boys wore a dull-colored, collarless, button-free, untucked-in tee shirt over equally drab pants. Failure to follow this unwritten dress code might bring a frown. The girls enjoyed more freedom, but what they wore was dictated by the group they hung out with, or rather by the leader of the group.

Ben saw all this and didn't like it. He liked bright colors and didn't see why he shouldn't wear what he wanted. Sam encouraged him to do just that. "It'll build character," he said. *Sounds like Abby talking,* Ben thought. But Maria had other ideas. "You stand out enough as it is. Blend in when you can. Save your energy for the important battles." Ben thought of consulting Granny but shut her out—he remembered Abby's warning. Anyway, on this particular day, as on most other days, Ben was wearing the drab "uniform."

One boy stood out on the playground because he refused to wear it. His wardrobe consisted of brightly colored shirts and white pants. On this day he wore a vivid blue-and-orange, buttoned Hawaiian shirt. He stood out in another way as well. He was profoundly obese. He was in Ben's Algebra class, and Ben already admired him for his bright mind. This boy's name was Ferdinand Aguirre. Ben's group stood about twenty feet from Ferd's group, composed of Ferd and three other smallish boys, when a larger, athletic-looking boy of mixed race walked up. This was Duvall Odom, and he wore on his face a hardened, arrogant look that Ben associated with gangs.

"I need your lunch money, Marshmellow," Duvall said to Ferd.

Ferd looked up at the taller boy and stammered, "I—I need it too."

"I said I need your lunch money, Spaz!"

Ben overheard Duvall the second time and turned to watch. He noticed a group of big boys standing off to the side and assessing the situation. They seemed to be with Duvall.

Ferd said, "But I—I—"

"Look here, you peacock, I need it *now*." Duvall grabbed Ferd's shirt in one hand and twisted it while staring his victim down.

"OK," said Ferd, close to tears. He reached under his shirt for his wallet.

"And if you tell anybody about this, you're dead meat. You got that, Fat Boy?"

Ben, looking on, felt his anger grow, but also his fear. He remembered Pam Grady at the birthday party and knew he ought to try to stop it, but he didn't want to fight. He feared getting his teeth knocked out or something worse, and he feared almost as much knocking the other kid's teeth out. He had never been in a fight before anyway. He calculated quickly. Could he beat the other boy in a fistfight? They were the same height, but the other boy was more muscular, probably a year older. And there were the others. But he thought of Pam again and wondered if Abby might be looking on now. He definitely didn't want to disappoint her. *Oh God!* he thought. He took a deep breath, sent up a quick prayer, and stepped out from the protection of his group.

"Let's settle this in some other way," he said as he positioned himself next to Duvall.

"Who are you?" said Duvall, momentarily surprised.

"It doesn't matter. Please give him his money back."

"Get out of my face!" Duvall pushed Ben back, and Ben hit the ground.

Startled but unhurt, Ben hatched an idea as he got up. He approached Duvall again. "I got a deal for you," he said. "You look pretty fast. But I bet I'm faster. I'll race you around the soccer goal over there and back. If I win, you give him his money back; if you win, you get my lunch money, too."

A surly smile spread over Duvall's face. "You know who you talkin' to, fool? I'm the point guard on the basketball team. You think you can beat me?" With a contemptuous grin he turned to his friends and said, "Hey, the fool thinks he can beat me in a race!"

His friends didn't respond. Ben wondered if they went along with what Duvall was doing.

"Hey, Norbert, hold the money."

"Now you gonna get it fair and square," said Norbert, the tallest of the boys.

Ben walked over to the group and held out the five-dollar bill that Maria had stuck into his wallet that morning. "Just in case I lose," he said.

"You gonna lose, all right," said Norbert.

The smile on Duvall's face gave way to an expression that was all business when he and Ben lined up side by side and aimed their bodies at the goal, about a hundred yards away. Norbert told one of his group to run ahead and clear the path. By now more than a hundred kids looked on, though most didn't understand what was at stake.

"You better beat him, Duvall! Because if you don't, don't expect any money from me. You ready?" Then Norbert recognized Ben. "Hey, aren't you the Ghost Boy?" He looked at his friends, slapped his knee, and laughed so hard he made everybody else laugh with him, except Ben and Duvall. "Hey Duvall, you racing the Ghost Boy! Ghosts can fly! You think you can beat him?" Again he just cracked up.

Norbert finally composed himself enough to tell the racers to take their mark. Then he held up his hand and sliced it down with the yell, "GO!"

Duvall and Ben ran neck and neck until they reached the soccer goal. Duvall had the inside, and Ben was forced to trail him around the turn. Now they were on the homeward stretch. Ben had been practicing basketball on the side and was in great shape. He was a natural born sprinter to begin with. He sprinted ahead of Duvall. In shame Duvall slipped into the crowd before he reached the finish line. Some of the crowd cheered Ben, especially Ferd and his little group.

"Hey, man, you pretty fast," said Norbert in his deep, husky voice as Ben came up out of breath to get his money back. Norbert respectfully handed him the bill, then said, "I'm glad you beat him. But you'll be hearing from him again. He pretty mean."

Ben discovered what it was like to keep an eye over his shoulder. When he and Duvall occasionally met in a hallway or the playground, Duvall looked at him with a sullen stare and said something like, "You'll be hearin' from me any day now, fool!" or just pointed a finger at him as he walked by. Ben understood first-hand why people often looked behind them when a car approached from the rear. For Ben, Duvall was the car. Still, nothing more might have come of the incident if it weren't for the basketball team.

The previous year Ben had been a starting forward for his school. He had been too tall to be the point guard, but in junior high he was just about right for that position, especially if he made the varsity squad. He remembered, though, that Duvall said he was the point guard.

Fifty boys tried out for the varsity basketball team, and after three weeks of gruelling practice Ben was given the choice of starting on the JV team or playing backup on the varsity team.

Ben thought about it hard and talked it over with his dad, then finally decided for varsity. It turned out that Duvall was indeed the point guard, and Ben would be his backup. The team was mostly mixed race, gifted, and well coached. Ben felt honored just to be a part of it. Norbert, who turned out to be the key player, the big guy "in the middle," seemed to take a fancy to Ben and even passed back to him in scrimmages; Ben returned the favor, looked for Norbert under the basket, and passed in to him when he could.

In scrimmages Ben and Duvall were usually on opposite sides since they played the same position, and they usually guarded each other. Duvall taunted Ben every chance he got. "Hey, Retard, one of your ears sticks out farther than the other," he said once. And Ben went home and discovered in the mirror for the first time that it actually did stick out a little farther. "Hey, Space Man, where'd you get that big head?" he said another time, referring to Ben's prominent forehead. It was one taunt after another.

Sometimes Duvall's tactics turned vicious. Once during practice Ben fell down and Duvall stepped on his head. The coach saw it and suspended Duvall for a practice, and Ben played on the first team in his place. But that only made Duvall hate all the more. At least once every practice Duvall tripped Ben when the coach was out of the gym or had his back turned talking to someone, and Ben would go sprawling.

Ben knew that talking to Duvall would do no good, or else he would have tried it a long time ago. He also knew that Duvall came from a home with no father and sometimes talked about joining a gang. He knew the only thing keeping Duvall out of trouble was basketball, and he was glad Duvall was a good basketball player playing on one of the best teams in the county. It was this understanding that kept Ben's fear of Duvall from turning to something like hatred. In fact there was one thing about Duvall that Ben liked. It wasn't his dribbling or passing skill, but his pity for a stray dog that happened to wander loose on the campus one night after practice. "I'm gonna take him home to my mom, or else he's gonna get picked up by the S.P.C.A.," Duvall said. Was it the love of his mother or the love of the dog, just a common brown street dog with a curly tail, which touched Ben more? Whatever it was, Ben liked Duvall better from that day on.

Duvall's hatred of Ben got the best of him one day in February as the team practiced for the last game of the regular season before the league championship tournament started. There was a loose ball, and Ben and Duvall both dived for it. Ben wrenched it away, and Duvall started swinging at Ben with his fist. Several of the blows found their mark, and blood spurted from Ben's nose. The coach saw it all and had warned Duvall several times before. He rushed up and pulled Duvall off Ben, who lay on the floor bleeding with the ball still in his grasp. "Get some towels!" he said. Then he stood up, all six foot five inches of him, and said to Duvall, "You and Ben will never play on the same team again. Now get out!"

On the next night Ben started the game at point guard while Duvall looked on from the stands. Ben had by far his best game ever, scoring six points and dishing out nine assists. Norbert, who had been on the receiving end of most of those assists and scored twenty-six points, told Ben after the game, "You not bad for a 7th grader," and then gave him a big, warm grin. Ben fell happily asleep that night not reliving the baskets he made, but thinking about that grin.

On Thursday morning before class started for the day, Ben sat alone in Coach Henry Jackson's office waiting for the coach to arrive. All around the room trophies stood—trophies in cases, trophies on stands, trophies on bookcases, several trophies even on the desk. Ben stood up and studied this last trophy, small and undistinguished, because it showed a girl pitching a softball. It stood next to pictures of his family and was labeled, "LaTanya Jackson, Most Valuable Player."

"Ben, what brings you here this morning?" Coach Jackson said in his most friendly voice as he walked through the door.

This was not the way Ben had hoped it would start. He could barely bring himself to say it. "Uh, Coach Jackson, I— uh—I de-decided—that I—need to drop off the team."

"Drop off the team?! Did I hear you right, Son?"

"Yes, I—it isn't right for me to play while Duvall sits."

"Drop off the team? You gotta be kiddin'!" Coach Jackson couldn't believe his ears. "What are you talkin' about?" An amazed smile broke over his face.

"It's Duvall, Coach," Ben tried to explain again. "I've talked to my parents and thought it through. It isn't right for me to play while Duvall sits."

"The hell it ain't! You don't think I know what's been goin' on? I even know the story. Ben, I've put up with Duvall long enough. I made my decision. I made it with you in mind! I did it *for* you. You're my man, Ben! Hey, didn't you have a good time last game?"

"I had a great time, Coach, but—"

"Then what's the problem?"

"I keep thinking about Duvall. I've been thinking about him all week."

"Duvall? After what he did to you? Why you worried about Duvall, Ben? What's really goin' on here?"

"Well, Duvall's better than me, and—"

"He's not that much better, and, besides, I can't go back on my word. It's finished! I'm just glad you did as well as you did. Frankly I was surprised. And you've looked good in practice this week. If you keep playing that way, we're not gonna miss Duvall that much."

"But, Coach, I'm not asking you to go back on your word. All you said was that Duvall and I couldn't play on the same team."

"Yeah, that was my way of kickin' his butt off the team."

Ben knew that, but he didn't let it distract him. "But if I step down, and he comes back, we won't be playing on the same team, and you won't be going back on your word."

Coach Jackson studied Ben from behind his desk and didn't say a thing. Then he asked very slowly, "Did Duvall threaten you?"

"No, Coach, this is my idea. Nobody's pressuring me."

Coach Jackson's good-natured dark face puckered up, and

he said, "Let me get this straight. This kid hates your guts, beats you up, and you like the guy so much you want to give him your job. Is that what you're sayin', Ben? Because that's sure as hell what it sounds like you're sayin'!"

Ben looked down into his lap and said, "Something like that. Yes, Sir, that's what I'm saying."

"But that don't make sense! Ben, look at me straight in the eye. Why are you doin' this?"

"Well, because I know how he's suffering. He saw the last game, and Norbert said he's been missing school this week. Coach, I've got so much going for me. I'm so lucky. And so are you." Ben looked down at the pictures on the desk. "But Duvall doesn't have a dad, and his mom's on drugs half the time. I've been thinking about this all week long. Coach, I hate to step down. When Norbert told me what a good job I did Friday, I was the happiest guy on earth. But just think of Duvall." Ben paused. "Do you understand why I want to step down, Coach?"

When Ben finished, Coach Jackson nodded his head slowly and said very deliberately, "I think I do. But I can't believe my ears." He stood up and said with deep emotion, "Ben, I don't like it, but I see your point. All I can say is I've never seen anything like this in all my long life. Come here, son."

Coach Jackson gathered Ben to himself and gave him a hug.

"So I can step down?" said Ben looking up at the big man standing close beside him.

Coach shrugged his shoulders, held his hands out to the side with palms turned upward, and said, "Who's gonna stop you?"

"And you'll let Duvall back on the team?"

Coach looked at Ben with his face puckered up and said, "You sure he's not bribing you or something?"

"No. No, Sir. I just want—"

"Oh, I know! I shouldn't have said that. It's just that…" He couldn't find words to say what he meant.

"I'll be at the game, Coach," Ben finally said. "I'll be your number one rooter! And I'll be your point guard *next* year."

"You sure will," said Coach. "You sure will."

As Ben got up to leave, Coach Jackson said, "Just a minute. I've been meaning to ask you. Do you really see ghosts like they say you do?"

"I used to."

"I ask because my littlest girl—she's the one over there"— he pointed to a family picture—"claims she does too. I never knew what to make of it. What do you advise me to do?"

Ben was not ready for this. All he could do was stammer stupidly, "Just enjoy it, Coach."

Coach Jackson looked at Ben for a moment without speaking, then said, "Well, I sure will."

When Ben left the office, big Henry Jackson locked the door and stared at the pictures of his family. After a couple of seconds he stifled a sob. "Hot damn!" he finally said loud enough for Ben to hear him through the door as he exited the outer office.

On the following Saturday afternoon, Ben sat high in the stands with his dad as a crowd gathered. When his former teammates came out on the floor to start their pre-game warm-up drills, he noticed something sewn on the back of Duvall's golden jersey inside his number, "00." Ben looked closely and saw the initials "BC" and "B" inside the first zero, and "C" inside the second. Five minutes into their drills, the players stopped what they were doing and, with Coach Jackson leading, scanned the stands on both sides. Suddenly one of them pointed at Ben and told the others where he was. The rest looked up at him and motioned for him to come down.

Feeling a little foolish, Ben made his way down to the floor.

All his teammates and the Coach met Ben near the bench. Duvall was in the middle of them, and everybody was looking at him. Duvall stepped out from the circle and said to Ben, "Hey, man, thanks."

The two adversaries looked at each other for a second, and Duvall saw something that said "It's OK" in Ben's eyes. He stammered, "Hey, man, I'm sorry for what I done to you."

Ben reached out his arms to Duvall and held him in a light embrace. His teammates gathered around the couple and held them in a bigger embrace.

They broke the huddle, and Duvall looked up one more time into Ben's eyes. He quickly brushed aside a tear, nodded once, and put on his best all-business basketball face.

Chapter 15

MEAN GIRL

Within a few days the name Juana Hidalgo was known all over the school. Few students knew her personally, but what happened to her on the school grounds was big news. She had been the leader of a tight group of girls going back to her elementary school days, and they had turned on her. There was a lot of shouting and then a fight, a big fight. Girls didn't usually settle things with fists, but this time they did. Clothes were torn off before teachers could break through the mob and break it up. No one could remember such a brawl. The excuse was a boy, but there was much more to it, and there was plenty of speculation going around. Smart phones lit up with text messages and the air crackled with gossip. When Juana went to school the next day, she had no friends. No one wanted to go anywhere near her; she was an untouchable. No one would speak to her except to ridicule her. She was a complete pariah.

Ben's friends wanted to see the legendary girl in the living flesh, like everyone else at school who didn't know her.

They got their chance on Thursday, five days after the fight. Ben, Jared, Adam, and six or seven other boys sat on the steps where they ate their lunch.

"There's that girl, that Juana what's-her-name," said Levi, the only boy in the group who knew her by sight. "Over there, sitting on the ledge, by herself." He pointed to her, about eighty feet away.

For the most part Ben didn't run with mean kids, and no

one in his group wanted to add misery to her lot; but they all followed her with their eyes, and she probably saw Levy point and the rest of the boys staring. She wore loose-fitting blue jeans and an ordinary white tank top. Her black hair hung down straight behind her back.

"You Juana, you gotta!" whispered Jared with a mischievous twinkle in his blue eyes as he eyed Ben. He knew of Ben's peculiar habit of stepping in and defending the weak. But Juana Hidalgo? Did Ben have the courage to come to *her* defense? Jared didn't think so. In fact, he hoped not. The other boys didn't know what to make of Jared's odd comment and let it pass.

But Ben didn't. From that moment he studied Juana and tried to screw up his courage. He remembered the Miller twins' cousin, Pam. He remembered Ferd and the lunch money. He remembered how Abby told him to stick up for the underdog and that it was "commendable." He knew what he should do, but he was afraid. But then he thought of Jared's dare, heard it ringing in his ear. Or was it an insult? With celery stalk in hand, he picked up his lunch bag and forced himself to walk over to Juana Hidalgo. As he got closer, he noticed that her face was a little pimply. She was far from beautiful, but neither was she plain. She looked half-Hispanic and half-Asian. She didn't look especially sexy or trashy. Her eyes were red, as if she had been crying. She ate alone and stared down at the ground.

He stood next to her and waited for her to look up. An overhanging tree partially shut out the sun, and shadows danced across the ledge where she sat.

She finally raised her head, and her eyelids fluttered in shame and fear. She lowered her eyes, stared at her food, and pretended he wasn't there.

Ben hadn't had time to think about what he would say. So all he said was, "Are you—are you—Juana?"

Juana did not look up at him. She knew what was coming. She'd heard it a hundred times before. Her face hardened, her eyes squeezing into slits and her jaw sticking out slightly. She stopped chewing but did not answer.

"My name's Ben Conover. I'm the guy they used to call Ghost Boy. I just wanted to say I'm sorry about what happened to you last week. And I know what it's like to be made fun of."

Her face did not look up, but her eyes did. She studied him with suspicion. He did not have a mean face; he looked at her with—no, it was the latest sick joke. She looked back down at the ground and hoped he would go away.

"I'll leave you alone if you want me to. But I know what it's like to be alone." He was thinking of his first few weeks on the basketball team before he was accepted.

"Leave me alone," she said.

Ben turned to go. But as he was turning she looked up and said, "What'd you say your name was?"

"Ben Conover."

"Are you that guy on the basketball team?"

"I was on the team, yeah."

"You're that guy who—who quit—so that other—that other guy could play?"

"Yeah. But it wasn't a big deal." He was surprised anybody knew. There had been a small article in the school bulletin two months earlier, that was all. "Can I sit down?"

She moved over to make room for him beside her. She studied him closely and still a little suspiciously. "You're not going to call me a—a name?"

"A name? Why would anybody do that?"

"Because they can. Because they hate me. And it isn't true."

He looked at her and felt her hurt. She must have felt his compassion because it melted her a little. She put her hands over her face and composed herself. Finally she said, "You must think I'm a fool. I'm sorry."

"A fool? Why? Not at all."

"You pity me, don't you?"

Ben had to think a moment. "Yeah, I guess I do. Is that all right?"

She looked up at him through her fingers. He leaned over and gently placed his hand on her forearm near the wrist, which propped up her face. She did not pull back.

The bell rang, and Ben looked over at his table. All his friends were staring at him. "Time to go, Ben," called one of them.

"See you around," he said to Juana.

They both got up and went to their classes.

Jared and Ben usually walked home from school together, and this afternoon was no different. Jared wanted to set Ben straight about Juana.

"Ben, even the guys in PE know about her. One of them saw you with her. She's already been dumped by her boyfriend, and you go over and sit with her."

"What's wrong with that?"

"That was stupid, Benji! Everybody hates her. And you go do something stupid like that. You even—*touched* her! Why did you do that?" Jared was angry.

Ben was angry too. Sitting with Juana was one of the hardest things he'd ever done, and Jared condemned him for it. "Why do *you* think I did it?"

"You tell me! Sometimes I think you're a little crazy. Look, you've got your reputation to worry about. We all do. Sometimes it's embarrassing to be your friend, Ben. Sometimes you're just not cool at all."

"So you really think I did it because I'm crazy."

"No, not really." Jared looked at his friend and squinted into the sun. "Then why *did* you do it? Why did you touch her?"

"Because it was the right thing to do, Jared."

"It was *not* the right thing to do! They're already making jokes about you."

"It *was* the right thing to do. It wasn't the cool thing to do, but it was the *right* thing."

"All I can see is you ate lunch with the school sleaze, and everybody knows about it!"

"You're wrong. That's just made up garbage."

"She deserves everything she gets! We all do. If I did what she did, I'd expect everybody to hate me too. And I'd deserve it."

"No, you wouldn't. We all mess up. We have to help each other when we mess up. You know that."

"So you were helping her. So when the guys ask me why my best friend ate with that slut, I'm supposed to say because he was helping her. Get real, Benji!"

"You don't get it, Jared. You keep coming back to what people think. *I don't care what people think.* All I care about is —"

"You really don't care what I think of you, Ben?"

"Of course I do. You're my friend. But I don't care what the rest of the world thinks. At least I try not to."

Jared and Ben walked along in silence. Jared was glad to hear Ben cared about what he thought. In fact he glowed over the news, for he really loved Ben. But he still hadn't conquered his jealousy of Adam. And that little green demon was about to get the better of him.

"You know what Adam said? He said you wanted to—make out with her. He told some guys that."

Ben exploded. "Adam? Adam—what? Adam would never say that! You're lying! I know you're lying!" Ben was shouting, and Jared was afraid of what he'd set loose. Jared was in fact lying. It was Jared himself who said what he was accusing Adam of, told it to the guys he had PE with. He was kidding around, of course. Sort of.

"Look," Ben continued, "I'm going to sit with Juana everyday, *everyday*, if she wants me to. Maybe you'd better look for a new friend!"

"Everyday? Well, your mom's a Mexican. You Mexicans stick together, I guess."

"What?! What are you talking about? You think it makes any difference—what are you? —difference to me—where she comes from? You just don't get it!" Ben quickened his pace, then broke into a run. His heavy backpack full of books flopped up and down on his shoulders. He felt utterly betrayed by his best friend. He tripped over a bump in the sidewalk and fell, skinning his knee. He got up and ran again. He felt angry. More than angry, he was in a blind rage. He wanted to call Jared every sick name he'd ever heard. They jangled around in his head, and he found himself saying them out loud, almost spitting them out, as he ran on. He forced himself to slow down, and his fury subsided. He thought of Juana and wondered what people would say if she kept coming to him. *Oh, God, don't let her come again,* he prayed. But then he felt ashamed. And he prayed, *Help me not to care what they think.* But he did care, he cared a lot, and he felt miserable. He came to the front gate of his house and passed under the great trees. He noticed a robin hopping on the lawn, looking for a worm. He saw it had only one leg, and he stopped to study it as it hopped around. It seemed to get along fine. He thought of Ferd Aquirre, the obese boy at school he had won the race against Duvall for. Like the jay, Ferd managed.

He took a last look at the robin and felt ashamed. He realized that what he would have to face over the next month or so was nothing compared to what Ferd faced every day of his life. He felt his courage return. If Juana wanted him to be her friend, then he would be her friend. That was all there was to it.

As he unlocked the front door, he felt a sort of calm fall over him. He dreaded what lay ahead of him, but at least he knew who he was, and he knew what he had to do.

Juana did come back, but not right away. A week passed. Then there she was, sitting on the same ledge and stealing glances at him. He had almost forgotten her and hoped she'd forgotten him. She nodded at him.

"Sorry, guys, I've got to go," he said.

"Oh my God!" said Jared.

On this day Juana Hidalgo told Ben the whole story as a mockingbird sang its heart out from the top of a nearby tree. Words poured out of her nonstop.

"I was the leader of my group and made the rules. You had to dress a certain way, talk a certain way, eat a certain way, wear your hair a certain way, text a certain way, tattoo a certain way, even study and cook a certain way. And if the rules didn't cover a situation, I made them up on the spot. I was their queen. You know what I mean?"

"Yeah, I guess."

"Sometimes I would dis one of the girls, especially if they were weak or violated one of the rules. They all feared me, and I made sure they did. But then I told Gabby she was out. I had warned her many times, but she just kept eating her stupid French fries and drinking her Pepsis. She just kept getting fatter and fatter. She was obese. I told her to leave."

Juana paused here and took a deep breath. A scowl painful to look at was scribbled across her face. She went on:

"Well, that's what started it. There was an argument, and then all of a sudden the whole group turned on me. They were like a pack of wild dogs. They beat me up. I'm sure you heard. They told my boyfriend I was a liar and a bully and that I controlled him like a puppet. Those bitches! Well, he hasn't spoken to me ever since. Then I tried to force myself back in. They told me to get lost and pushed me away. You should see the texts I got. Like 'Die loser!' The ones I knew still liked me even joined in. God! I forced them to study—that was one of the rules I most enforced. And they did, and their grades improved. They owe me. You have no idea how much they owe me! But I'm all alone. No friends. Unwanted." She had begun to sob.

"But you have a family."

"Family?! My dad's in Lerdo prison. My mother holds down a job as a waitress, but she has a drinking problem. She says she loves me all the time, but she loves the bottle more. That leaves my brother. He'd kill for me, and I do mean that literally. He's like me in a way. He controls a group of guys. They're like a gang. They do what he tells them."

Ben had no idea what to say, and two more weeks passed. He almost forgot about her.

"Can I talk to you?" This time she came right up to his group and said these words to Ben in a humble, almost sweet tone.

Ben left the safety of his group once more, and this time Juana had a totally different story.

"I want to tell you I've been seeing Mrs. Bannister, you know, the counsellor? Anyway, she helped me. Look—there they are—over there."

She pointed to a group of about ten girls chattering away and enjoying themselves out in the sun.

"I don't hate them anymore."

"Really? You really don't? What happened? That's awesome. Why not?"

She took a deep breath and sighed. "I'm the bitch, not them. They're just weak. Mrs. Bannister told me to do a Google search on Mean Girls." Do you know about Mean Girls?

"No."

"I was the classic Mean Girl. They do whatever is necessary to control their group. Anything. You understand? Anything. Threaten, start vicious rumors, exclude. I was a big-time excluder. I let girls into the group and forced others out. And to stay in the group they'd do everything I told them. I began to get high on all that power. It amazed me. It was fun making them do silly things. One day I told them all to wear orange socks the next day, and they did! I was like a tyrant, a dictator. No wonder they hated me. I for sure saw myself in those articles. And it was like a revelation. I hated myself more than they did. But when I finally understood what happened to me, I felt a kind of relief. I turned myself into a monster, and now I saw what I had to do. And I was glad they threw me out. Except that now I'm so alone. I even went back to apologize, but they wouldn't accept it."

"You apologized? You're kidding. Wow, that's awesome."

"And I want to apologize to you. For being so terrible."

"To me? What did you ever do to me? You're not terrible at all. You're, you're amazing! You can be my friend anytime."

"No, you're too good, too innocent. You don't deserve a friend like me."

"No. No. That's not true."

That's when Ben started to sit with Juana in the lunch room. He was won over by her humility. He was beginning to find her attractive.

It wasn't long before Juana grew to love Ben more than she had ever loved any friend before. He was young, almost a year younger. She was right: he was innocent, she could tell. She restrained her natural urge to snuggle with him, and the restraint felt right and good. It gave her self-respect, and she found herself able to pray at night. When she prayed, she poured out her heart in thanksgiving for Ben, and she felt clean and happy. One of the girls in her old group asked if she wanted to study together, and another gave her a call at home. Her complexion even got better.

With her new self-respect, she gained courage. And she would need it for the thing she was about to do. She decided to cook a dinner for Ben. That way he could see what a good cook she was and he could meet her family, meaning her mother and brother. She knew he was from a good family and lived in a good neighborhood in the southwest, and all she could claim was a humble house on the eastside. But she was determined, someday, to marry Ben—that was her goal, crazy as it might be. This was to be the start of the plot.

Juana looked good when she met him at the door. She

wore a pleated blue skirt that came down just above her knees and a soft silky white blouse. She had applied mascara and lipstick in exactly the right places, and her brown eyes were happy and almost radiant. Ben had never seen her like this.

"Wow! You look great," he said.

Juana introduced him to her mother, who came up to the front door right behind Juana. He was too taken with the new Juana to take much notice of the shortish, fleshy woman with a healthy mane of black hair streaked with gray gathered in a loose bun, and small gold earrings that dangled to her neck. The "nice to meet yous" were passed around.

The good beginning didn't last long. Ben could tell as soon as he walked into the living room that something wasn't right. There was an oppressive feeling that overtook him despite his resolve to keep his "gift" bottled up; the house felt haunted. He was just starting to look around to see what was there when Juana's brother walked up.

"Ben, this is my brother, Miguel."

Ben and Miguel stared at each other in disbelief. Their mouths hung half open in a kind of dreadful astonishment.

"Are you...Dingo?" said Ben.

"You're the kid...?"

"You know each other?" said Juana in surprise.

Ben looked at Juana in confusion. "His name is? —I knew him as Dingo."

"His real name is Miguel. You know my brother?"

"Oh man, this ain't real!" said Miguel. "Hey, man, I feel bad. I feel *bad!*"

"What's going on?" said Juana. "Ben, what's going *on?*"

"Yeah, we know each other," said Ben, looking down at the carpet.

"From where?"

"Oh man, I'm sorry," Miguel said. "I'm sorry, man. After what you did for my sister."

"It's all right," said Ben. "That was a long time ago."

"Oh man!" Miguel kept repeating.

"What happened?!" Juana pleaded.

"It's in the past. It doesn't matter. I forgive you. Forget it."

At the word "forgive" Juana became quiet. She knew that something serious had happened between Ben and her brother. She respected their need for privacy and stepped back.

"I owe you one, man," said Miguel. "What can I do for you?" His eyes were still averted. He couldn't stand looking at Ben face to face.

"I want to do something, something for you. For what you did for my sister. She's a different girl since she met you."

Ben looked at Miguel for a few seconds and wondered what to say. Then he remembered the jackknife, its blade flashing under the sun next to the flagpole. He remembered the sickening fear he felt.

Ben sucked in a deep breath and said, "Well, maybe there's something you can do for me. Something special. Do you remember the jackknife? Would you give that to me, you know, as a gift?"

Miguel looked at Ben with his mouth speechless and slightly open. He looked up at Ben for the first time and said, "Oh man, not that. Not that. That knife is my buddy. We've traveled a long way together. It's my buddy. One time this dude gave me the finger and I caught him and cut off his middle finger with that knife. He won't be giving anybody the finger anytime soon! No, man, not my buddy. Please.

What else?"

Ben looked at Miguel but didn't back down. He remained silent.

"Hey, Sis," Miguel said, "I gotta go. Have a good time." He almost rushed out the front door. You could hear the car screech down the street in full flight.

Juana fell onto the couch and was sobbing. When Ben came over to comfort her, she pushed him away and beat her hand onto a cushion. Now she sobbed uncontrollably. Her mother quietly drifted into the kitchen.

What could Ben say? That he loved her for who she was and that she was not her brother? Could he tell her that the feeling of oppression that had been in the house when he entered was gone? He remembered that strange thing that clung to Dingo in the park. Had the family been living with it in their own home ever since, and maybe much longer? Could he tell her a dark spirit left the house with her brother?

Juana served up a nice chicken dinner, but the evening was ruined, her plans, her dreams smashed.

When Ben left, he gave her a quick hug, then let her go. She clung to him for an extra moment, then let go herself.

She looked up at him and said in a voice that wavered, "Thanks for a beautiful friendship. I'll never forget what you did for me. I love you, Ben. I always will. It's so perfect the way it is."

She reached out with her arms one more time and gave him an almost violent squeeze, then turned back through the door.

Two days later Maria met a tall older boy at the door who held a cloth shopping bag.

"Is Ben here?" he said, not looking at her. Maria didn't much like the look of him.

"No, he's at baseball practice. Why?"

"Here, give him this. He'll know what it's about."

"OK." She took the bag. "And who are you?"

He looked down at her for an instant, then looked away. "He'll know." He turned around and hurried down the curved walkway leading toward his car.

Maria was appalled when she turned the bag upside down. "What in the world!" she said. Out tumbled a jackknife and a sealed envelope. "What in the world has my Ben gotten into now?"

She carefully opened the envelope and read the following note: "Dear Ben, We are sorry and we are going to change our ways. Miguel, Sidney, Crawfish, Marcus (Mustard)." And then at the very bottom, scrawled in a different hand, was the message, "Remember me? Good luck! Marcus."

When Ben came back from baseball practice, he explained everything to his mother, then asked, "Was Juana with him?"

"No, unless she was in the car."

"And there was no other note?"

"No, just this." She pointed to the boys' note.

Ben was disappointed. He knew Juana had reasons for her silence, but he missed her.

That summer he wondered why she never called. He often thought of calling her, but always remembered her last words, "It's so perfect just the way it is."

He would never see Juana Hidalgo again.

Chapter 16

THE INTERVIEW

The time had come for Ben to bring up the subject of his birth. It was his 13th birthday, and this was his D-Day. He had waited a year, and Mom and Dad had said nothing about it. He wondered why Abby ever thought they might.

But he was hopeful. Abby had secretly visited him a month before and given him the key to the "proof," the key that her heavenly mentors had constructed ever so carefully, the key designed to open his father's mind and force acceptance. But Ben had no way of knowing if the key would actually work. And her mentors had no way of knowing the future.

So Ben was anxious to know how his parents would handle the revelation. He thought there was a good chance they'd deny every word of it. He even found himself doubting it, even though at the time he was absolutely sure it was true. Could it be that Abby had dreamed the whole thing up to get close to him?

He realized that not just his parents were on trial, but Abby too. He also realized that there was no foolproof way of getting at the truth if his parents denied the story. They might be completely sincere, or they might be covering up the truth. If they did, there would be no way to learn what was true. He hoped and prayed they would come clean. He dreaded the thought that Abby's story was false. It would mean there was a chance not only that he imagined the whole story but Abby herself. And it might even mean he was crazy after all, the scariest thought of all.

He hadn't seen or spoken to Abby in a month, and that made him all the more unsure. But he had taken her advice to heart, maybe too much to heart. Abby's world had begun to fade as his own shone more brightly. He didn't want that to happen. He didn't want to lose his gift. He wanted to get control of it, to subdue it, not lose it.

So there was a lot riding on what he thought of as the "interview."

"Mom, Dad, can we talk?"

Both were puzzled by their son's serious demeanor, and they couldn't imagine what was coming.

They were sitting around the kitchen table, close to each other. The breakfast dishes had been put away and the "Happy Birthdays" said. The aroma of coffee filled the room.

"Dad, Mom, this is hard for me to say." Silence.

"Well, out with it," said Sam. "Say it straight out, whatever it is. You're going to tell us you're gay?"

"No, that would be too easy."

"Oh my God!" Maria said.

"I'm exaggerating." He paused and wriggled in his chair. Then, "Well, you remember Abby."

"I thought you were done—done with that," said Sam. "You haven't brought her up in a long time. Is she back?"

"No she's not."

"Then—what's the problem?"

"Well, last year we had a long talk. It was last summer at the bay house. I didn't tell you about it because she asked me not to. She asked me to wait a year. She wondered if you might tell me first."

"Tell you what?" Maria said.

"What are you talking about?" said Sam.

"Well, she told me the most amazing thing. She told me that I had a twin, a girl twin, who died before she was born. Mom, is this true?"

Maria and Sam looked at each other. Maria's lips moved slightly as if trying to convey something secretly to Sam. A frown wrinkled her smooth bronze forehead. Sam shook his head ever so slightly. Ben took it all in.

Maria looked as if she was in shock. She stared down at the table and was as still as stone. If she breathed, no one could tell.

"Ben," began Sam, "how could Abby know such a thing even if she's real? Why would you believe such a thing?"

"I don't exactly believe it. I'm just asking. *Is it true?*"

Sam rubbed the top of his head as he usually did when perplexed. Then he said, "Don't you think we'd have told you if it was?"

In desperation Ben turned to Maria. "Mom, *is it true?*"

She looked up at him, then at Sam. She moved her lips again.

"If you must," said Sam, looking at his wife.

She looked back at Ben and said almost in a whisper, "It is true, Son. It is."

"It is? Oh, I'm so relieved! Oh, thank you for telling me this! Thank you! But why did you keep it secret?"

Maria put her hands in front of her face and took a deep breath that sounded like a repressed sob violently bursting free. Then she shook her head.

"Your mother blames herself for that loss, which is absurd," said Sam quietly. He reached over and stroked Maria on the arm. "Our baby girl had been dead inside your Mom for three months, and the Doctor thought it best to let nature take its course. He said the fetus would come out as a blob of tissue at delivery. 'Blob of tissue,' those were his exact words. Anyway, he was wrong. She weighed only six ounces and was gray colored, but she came out with every finger and toe. The only thing missing was an eye; it had decomposed. Your mom and I and Granny and your Mom's mother took turns holding her. We held her for two hours. Then I brought her to the mortuary to be cremated. You came out first and were normal in every way."

"Mom, that's horrible! But what did you do—wrong?"

Maria was sobbing too much to answer.

"Nothing at all," broke in Sam. "She fell on her tummy going up the stairs. She was taking the laundry basket up. The doctor said that had nothing to do with it. He was adamant about that."

Ben stood up and hugged his mom from behind. Maria, still sobbing, stroked his hand.

"So you didn't tell anyone."

"Because it was too painful," said Sam. Then he looked at Ben, who rested his chin on his mother's head. "And you say the ghost girl told you this?" Then Sam looked at Maria. "Honey, did you tell anyone about this? I thought we agreed—"

"I told Carmen. After all, she's my sister! Only Carmen. And I told her not to tell anyone. I made her swear."

"Yeah, but how can you be sure she didn't pass the story on to Manny or Bernie? And maybe—"

"No, Dad. Believe me. I swear to you by everything I hold sacred. Nobody told me anything. Except Abby. Abby told me to tell you it had something to do with the placenta. I don't know exactly why. But that's what she said, *placenta*. She also said you would understand."

Maria's eyes grew round with excitement. "Sam, the placenta. The placenta! Remember?"

Sam leaned back in his chair as if thunderstruck. "The placenta? She said it was the placenta? Is that right, Ben?"

"That's right. Something to do with the placenta. Whatever that means."

"Well I'll be damned."

"What, Dad?"

It was Maria who spoke. "The cords were attached to the placenta at almost exactly the same place. Your baby sister didn't get enough oxygen and nourishment because you took it all."

"So why do you blame yourself?" Sam said to Maria. "You heard what the doctor said. You were in no way the cause of that."

Were they going to argue? "So Abby was right, Dad," Ben jumped in. "And there's more. Get this, Dad: Abby *was* that twin. That's how she knew, Dad. She was *there.*"

Sam's expression was hard to read. It seemed a blend of horror and elation and outright disbelief.

Maria's eyes glistened. "Abby is our baby girl? Your Abby? She's not dead? And she's grown up? She's your age? And she visits you? That is too much. But wait." She recollected something. "I knew it. Every year on the Day of the Dead I called her down and felt her presence. But I called her Eliza."

"Did you see her, Mom?"

"No. I don't see spirits. I just can feel them when they're around."

"And that's not all, Mom. Someday, when I get married,

I'm going to bring Abby into the world, into the family. I'm going to be her dad. She asked me to. I agreed. She's going to be your granddaughter, Mom!"

"Oh my God!"

"Hold on a minute," said Sam. "Let's not get carried away. All of this is completely amazing, and I want to believe it. But, Ben, you're talking about the future. You're saying that an invisible person that nobody else can see is describing a future that no one can know."

"No, it's not like that. She said there are other ways—other ways she can get back to earth. She doesn't know the future. This is just the way she hopes it will turn out. All I can say is I'll keep my side of the bargain. That's all I can say." Then he gave his dad a quizzical look. "Don't you believe in her now?"

Sam fiddled with his beard, stared down at the table, and shook his head. And shook his head some more. And some more.

"Oh, I forgot to tell you. She told me she loves you both very much."

Chapter 17

THE BIRTHDAY PARTY

It was later the same day, and the family gathered to celebrate Ben's 13th birthday in a more formal way. Aunt Carmen came with Manny and Bernie. Sarah, now 17, baked her first cake, chocolate with chocolate frosting.

Manny walked on his new plastic foot like he was born with it. He didn't limp and it didn't squeak. He didn't get a scholarship to USC, but he was content to start out at Bakersfield College as one of thousands of uncelebrated freshmen. Ben had been itching to tell him about the foot buried in the back yard and even thought of telling him exactly where it was. He hated secrets. But he decided to button his lips.

Adam had replaced Jared as Ben's best friend and was the only outsider at the party. He carried with him two nicely wrapped gifts, a chess set and a biography of Einstein written for teens. Ben had never beaten Adam at chess in at least a dozen tries, and Adam thought it might help if Ben had his own chess set. But Ben's payback was Scrabble. Adam had never beaten Ben in Scrabble, though he once came within a point. They loved those games as much as video games.

There was one other guest. Ben saw her off to the side just as the cake was being cut. She looked — was it sad? She didn't look at Ben but at the family gathered around the dinner table.

Ben got up and signaled to his mom to join him in the kitchen.

"She's here, Mom."

"Who?"

"Abby. She's here."

"Oh my God! Where?"

"In the dining room, just looking on."

"Should I tell your dad?"

He thought for a few seconds. "Tell him later."

They joined the others, and Abby was still there, just her face. She was smiling. Now she looked at him, looked at him in her strangely loving way and sent out a "happy birthday." She hovered just under Granny's portrait opposite the windows. Suddenly he remembered that this should have been a birthday party for her too. He didn't know what to feel or what to say. It was too late anyhow. She faded away like a snowflake touching the sea.

After Maria, Manny and Bernie had said their good nights, Ben and Adam decided to play one game each of Scrabble and Chess. "We played a lot of Monopoly growing up," Sam said as he brought out the card table. You boys wouldn't stand a chance against me."

"Aw, Dad, that's a kid's game," said Ben.

"Don't you believe it!"

Ben noticed that his dad had a strangely happy expression on his face. It suggested some secret puzzle solved.

That night Adam beat Ben at Scrabble for the first time. He did it on the last play of the game by spelling the word "dork." Ben challenged the word but was surprised to find it in the dictionary. The final score was 238 to 236.

"*You're* the dork," Ben said.

"And you're the weirdo," Adam shot back.

"Schmuck."

"Jerk."

"Retard."

"Geek."

"Nerd."

"Stoonch."

"Stoonch? What's a stoonch?" said Ben.

"Look it up in your Einstein book," said Adam.

"Einstein talked about a stoonch? You're kidding."

Adam looked at Ben and kept a straight face until he couldn't hold it anymore.

"You and your stoonch!" said Ben.

And they both laughed, and laughed, and laughed some more.

**OUR STREET
BOOKS**

Our Street Books
JUVENILE FICTION, NON-FICTION, PARENTING

Our Street Books are for children of all ages, delivering a potent
mix of fantastic, rip-roaring adventure and fantasy stories to excite
the imagination; spiritual fiction to help the mind and the heart;
humorous stories to make the funny bone grow; historical tales to
evolve interest; and all manner of subjects that stretch imagination, grab attention, inform, inspire and keep the pages turning.
Our subjects include Non-fiction and Fiction, Fantasy and Science
Fiction, Religious, Spiritual, Historical, Adventure, Social Issues,
Humour, Folk Tales and more.
If you have enjoyed this book, why not tell other readers by post-
ing a review on your preferred book site.

Recent bestsellers from Our Street Books are:

Relax Kids: Aladdin's Magic Carpet
Marneta Viegas
Let Snow White, the Wizard of Oz and other fairytale characters show you and your child how to meditate and relax. Meditations for young children aged 5 and up.
Paperback: 978-1-78279-869-9 Hardcover: 978-1-90381-666-0

Wonderful Earth
An interactive book for hours of fun learning
Mick Inkpen, Nick Butterworth
An interactive Creation story: Lift the flap, turn the wheel, look in the mirror, and more.
Hardcover: 978-1-84694-314-0

Boring Bible: Super Son Series 1
Andy Robb
Find out about angels, sin and the Super Son of God.
Paperback: 978-1-84694-386-7

Jonah and the Last Great Dragon
Legend of the Heart Eaters
M.E. Holley
When legendary creatures invade our world, only dragon-fire can destroy them; and Jonah alone can control the Great Dragon.
Paperback: 978-1-78099-541-0 ebook: 978-1-78099-542-7

Rise of the Shadow Stealers
The Firebird Chronicles
Daniel Ingram-Brown
Memories are going missing. Can Fletcher and Scoop unearth
their own lost history and save the Storyteller's treasure from the
shadows?
Paperback: 978-1-78099-694-3 ebook: 978-1-78099-693-6

Readers of ebooks can buy or view any of these bestsellers by
clicking on the live link in the title. Most titles are published in
paperback and as an ebook. Paperbacks are available in
traditional bookshops. Both print and ebook formats are
available online.

Find more titles and sign up to our readers' newsletter at
http://www.johnhuntpublishing.com/children-and-young-adult
Follow us on Facebook at https://www.facebook.com/JHPChildren
and Twitter at https://twitter.com/JHPChildren